AFTER THE SUFFRAGETTE'S SUICIDE

ETTA FAIRE

Website: http://ettafaire.com/

Join my list here

My author page with my other books

❀ Created with Vellum

CHAPTER 1

DEAD CLIENTS ARE SO DEMANDING

*W*orking with dead people has taught me that death is a part of life. Living with dead people has made me seriously wish there was a way to kill dead people.

That's what went through my head as I snooped around the library that afternoon, something I was absolutely certain went against the strict 75-page agreement I had to sign when I inherited this Victorian two months ago. But so far, my only regret was my shoe choice.

Those damn designer, light brown, ankle booties. I had to have them when I saw them sitting on the clearance rack, lonely and forgotten. Of course, they weren't in my section. Nothing good was ever in my section. Why did the whole world have to have a size 8?

"They're way too small," Shelby said, when she saw me twisting my foot at a strange angle to get them on. "You look like you're in pain."

"They just need to be broken in, is all," I said, because they were only ten dollars.

And now, I was breaking them in while trying not to break my neck. The library's rolling ladder swayed a little as I tried to stand on it while simultaneously running a hand along the dusty top shelf. My toes were numb and my foot slid forward every time I shifted my weight, because apparently, traction isn't included in ten-dollar shoes. But I was determined to snoop. And I figured the top shelf had to be where all the dirtiest secrets were.

I tugged another antique book from its spot, and looked it over. *Little Women.*

"Really?" I said to no one. "You hid Little Women, from who... women?"

I shook its pages with my free hand to see if anything good was hidden there, my feet slipping out from under me as I did. I grabbed the ladder just in time.

"Oh for goodness sakes, you're going to kill yourself snooping around like that," my ex-husband said, suddenly appearing in the desk chair below me. His coloring seemed strong in the afternoon light streaming in through the stained-glass windows. I could make out the dimple just above his beard. He looked up. "You could've at least worn a skirt. Made things interesting for a lonely ghost."

"Just as disgusting as ever," I said, realizing I hadn't even jumped when his ghost appeared. I was getting used to him popping in, which was a good thing; I could easily have fallen in these shoes, again. "And just so you know, dirty old men aren't considered adorable relics anymore. They're considered sexual harassers."

"But... adorable sexual harassers."

"If adorable includes getting fired, having their careers ruined, or, if they're a ghost, watching as their ex-wife sparks up the sage." I put the book back on the shelf and carefully climbed down, one step at a time, staring at my slippery, cute feet the whole way.

I jumped from the last step and my landing shook the entire

unstable turret, reminding me that this house was designed by a crazy man back before permits and safety were a priority.

"What are you looking for, anyway?" Jackson asked.

"Secrets."

"You'll have to be a lot more specific than that around here."

I sat down on the bright red sofa at the far end of the library and tugged off my boots, watching as my feet expanded to their natural form, like clowns from a tiny car. I opened the scrapbook in front of me on the coffee table. It was the one I'd found two months ago in this very room after the house helped me escape death.

And that scrapbook had set me on a quest to find out everything I could about the Victorian I'd inherited from my dead ex-husband, and the curse I'd apparently inherited along with it.

It probably wasn't a coincidence that I looked exactly like Eliza, the woman who had allegedly cursed the house in the early 1900s. From our curly light hair to the shape of the mole on our neck, we were the same. We even looked the same naked. I only knew that last part because the scrapbook in front of me had a photo on the last page of Eliza dancing nude on Henry Bowman's desk way back when.

But so far, that was about all I'd found out about the curse, other than the fact that I probably had a ghost for a housekeeper and a dog that seemed to be aging like Benjamin Buttons.

I closed the book before my perverted ex could ask to have a look at that last page or something, and ran my finger along the gold-embossed title: *There Was a Crooked Man*. Henry Bowman had been a crooked man, all right, making his millions off of shady brothels.

"I was actually hoping to find more books like this one," I said.

Jackson glanced at the cover, his arms crossed to reveal the pretentious, ridiculous elbow patches on his jacket. "So, you want my help in your snooping?"

"I'm not snooping. I'm exploring my own house. Now, did

you show up to annoy me? Because I don't have time." I looked at my cell phone to emphasize this, realizing I really didn't have time. *Shoot.* I had to be at the Purple Pony in an hour.

Jackson was just as snotty as usual. "Not that I need a reason to haunt my own house, but I actually have a bit of an announcement to make."

"You're ready to move on to a better place. I've heard that happens with dead people. See you later," I said.

"I could never do that to you, darling," he replied. "You'd be so lonely without me. Actually, I made a decision about our first client."

"Finally."

He'd been interviewing entities for the last two months, trying to decide who was worthy to be the first. I was getting a little tired of hearing about it.

He went on. "It's an honor to work with her, really. One of the oldest ghosts in Potter Grove has requested our services. Bessie Hind. She remembers my great grandfather, dear thing. Lots of stories to tell us about him, I'm sure."

I sat on the edge of my seat. Just the mention of Henry Bowman had me interested. "What on earth does she want with a channeling, though?"

Our services had come to mean a channeling, which is an odd kind of experience where an apparition enters your body and connects with your living energy. They can take you to any day in his or her memory, and you experience it exactly the way they did — the sights, sounds, tastes, feelings. Three months ago, when I did my first channeling with Jackson, I was able to use the clues I observed to help solve the murder of some local women. I also got to eat an incredible steak.

"This ghost has been dead for a while," I said. "She can't have any connections to the living anymore. What does she want with a channeling?"

Jackson flew behind me, a wash of cold shot up my spine as he rushed toward the short stack of books partially hidden by the sofa I was sitting on.

So that's where all the good books were.

After pulling off a large leather black one with gilded writing on its spine, just like the one on the table, he returned to the sofa.

"You've been holding out on me," I said, pointing to the scrapbook.

He licked his finger to scan over the pages, even though there could not have been any spit to help the process.

"Do you know where any other scrapbooks are," I asked.

"No, sorry. Just the one." The pages blew through his fingertips. "I do know my great grandfather kept many scrapbooks, though. This is the one dedicated to his social gatherings, I think. Who knows? The old man was eccentric."

Jackson's almost-transparent finger stopped on an old society newspaper clipping. At the top was a black and white photo of a beautiful, young, light-haired woman with pale skin and doe eyes, staring off in the distance. She wasn't smiling, but no one ever did in early photographs. The date said the article came from 1906. The caption: Socialite Bessilyn Margaret Hind commits suicide.

"You would think she'd remember committing suicide," Jackson said. "I'm sure that has to be memorable."

I ignored my ex-husband's attempt at a joke and read out loud:

During her thirty-fifth birthday celebration at the home of her parents, Miss Hind suggested to her many guests that she would be taking a long trip and that this would be farewell for a while. Following cake and champagne, the socialite retired to her room alone where she was later found shot in the chest.

Due to the fact that she was found alone, and her room door and window had been locked, police determined the death to be a suicide. Friends and family say she was despondent over a recent break-up with

Sir Walter Timbre of Landover and had confided that she was worried her chances at matrimony had passed her by.

Miss Hind was a champion for women's rights in Landover County, most notably the controversial suffrage movement, and is survived by both her parents, Greta and James Hind and her sister, Mrs. Pleasant Brillows.

"Poppycock!" a loud voice in front of us said.

I looked up, not the least bit surprised to see the same woman from the photo in the newspaper. She was a little older than she'd looked in the article, but then, the dead rarely got to choose what picture was put in their obituary. She was dressed in a silky champagne-colored dress, probably her party dress that evening, and her hair was in a loose up-do. Beautifully Edwardian looking. She was more colorful than Jackson. I could almost see the pink in her cheeks and the blonde highlights shimmering in the overhead light.

"Bessilyn, I presume," I said.

"I want retractions," she demanded before I had a chance to even ask what she was hoping to get from our channeling. "That obituary is rubbish and I want a full retraction, pronto."

"I'm not sure they do full retractions on obituaries, but even if they did, probably not on ones more than, say, a hundred years old."

She studied my face while she floated this way and that, inspecting it. I couldn't get over how much more lifelike she was than Jackson, and he was pretty colorful today. She touched my cheek and I actually felt her cold hand vibrating over it. "You look familiar," she finally said when she'd finished studying every crack in my makeup. "When I first saw you at the Purple Pony, I noticed it. And now that I'm getting an up close and personal look, I'm sure."

I nodded, slowly. "Well, I have become quite popular among

the ghosts in town, or so I've been told." I shot my ex-husband a look.

"Sorry, Carly doll. I should've mentioned she was here," he said. "She came from the bed and breakfast."

Bessie sat down on the desk chair. I'd never seen a straighter back or a more proper leg cross. "The Landover Bed and Breakfast used to be the Hind Estate, my family's home. The new owner is horrible. Paula Henkel. Dreadful, dreadful person who drives like she's asleep and snores like she's attempting to wake the dead."

"I heard the bed and breakfast is haunted. Now, I guess, I know whose work it is."

She patted her puffy hairline. "Thank you. I'll admit I had to increase my theatrics in order to get Miss Henkel to request a seance with your boss." She looked up at the ceiling. "The antics perfectly respectable ghosts must go through to impress the skeptics. Really."

"So you'd like retractions," Jackson interrupted, rolling his eyes. "What is it you can offer?"

"I can tell you think retractions are foolish," she said. She moved closer to my husband, making him back away. Jackson once told me ghosts couldn't get too close to each other. It was like two magnets trying to get together on the same polar end. They repelled and weakened one another.

It was obvious who the stronger ghost was here. She continued. "But I was a women's rights leader. And believe it or not, I was quite aware I was making history at the time I was making it. I cannot have people thinking I committed suicide over a man. It simply did not happen. Therefore, I want you to figure out who my murderer was, and, yes, I want full retractions on every piece of literature that talks about my suicide." She rubbed her gloved hands together. "Shall we get started?"

Jackson held his hand up. "Hold on a second, Bessie. We

talked about this. Carly needs to agree to the channeling. They're very hard on the living. Tell us what we'll get in return."

"Of course," she said. She hovered closer to me, studying my face again, turning her head this way and that. I could feel her heavy energy, and I gulped thinking about a channeling with such a strong ghost, especially one I didn't know. My boss at the hippie shop warned me not to do them at all, that they were harder on my body than I realized.

She finally spoke. "I was going to offer you a glimpse of Henry Bowman from 1906. He was at my party that night. But I think I can do better." Bessilyn was so close to my face I was surprised I didn't smell her perfume. "Because now I remember where I know you from," she said. "You're Henry Bowman's nanny. Or, you look just like her. Eliza, I believe. She was at my party, too, following the Bowmans around as usual, only there weren't any children with the Bowmans that evening. Hardly a need for a nanny, wouldn't you say?"

"Done," I said. "We'll do the channeling tomorrow."

CHAPTER 2

THE TROUBLE WITH UNICORNS

The six-foot-wide, glittery unicorn hanging above the front door of the Purple Pony was laughing at me again. My boss, Rosalie, claims the thing is good luck. She painted it years ago after she and her long-time boyfriend broke up just after college. She says it symbolizes new beginnings, strength, and courage to find your path in life. To me, it symbolizes an unnatural love for glitter and a minimum-wage job.

And right now it was mocking me for working here. Something my mother and the unicorn had in common.

Rosalie called to me from the back room when she heard me come in. I snaked my way around the racks of brown suede fringed dresses and turquoise beads to get to her voice. She was sitting at her desk, holding her calendar.

"Did I tell you about the seance we have coming up?" she said, tapping at the paper in her hand.

"The one at the bed and breakfast?"

"I did tell you."

"Nope, but my dead houseguest did." I hugged her hello. The large 60-year-old woman with graying dreadlocks and a wrinkle-free complexion was my boss but she was more like a second mom.

"Damn. If we sold tickets to your life, we'd make a fortune."

I loved Rosalie. She was all about *us* making a fortune off *my* freak show.

I didn't tell her the part where Bessilyn was my first client. Rosalie didn't approve of me channeling with ghosts, especially not for free. She didn't think it was worth it to be paid in secrets. I looked down at my cheap boots currently cutting the circulation off from my toes. She might have had a point.

I looked up. Rosalie was handing me a thick white book with nothing but two photos on its cover: a vintage black-and-white aerial shot of total dirt on the left and a current colorful one on the right of dirt and a few buildings. It was titled *Landover County: Then and Now*

"The new owner of the bed and breakfast loaned that to me. Turn to the page on her house. She wants us to be familiar with Bessilyn Hind."

"I'm very familiar with the suffragist," I said.

"Let me guess. Your dead houseguest. Why am I not surprised?" She pulled out the seance box from under her desk, which was just a regular cardboard box with some moons painted on it. She plopped it on her desk and pulled out its contents: a crystal ball, candlesticks, a deck of cards...

"If you can believe it," she said, gesturing with her EMF reader. "Paula wants us to come over to her bed and breakfast and confirm that this ghost is Bessilyn Hind after we close up shop today. As in, she will only pay us for the seance once we sign paperwork confirming what ghosts will be there. I've never heard of such a thing. Have you? What do you think she's up to?"

I shrugged. "That's weird. How much are we making off this?"

"Two hundred."

"A piece?"

"Total."

"There's no way we can know what ghosts are going to show up to a seance. Not for two hundred." I laughed. "That's not even worth pretending." I flipped through the pages. The paper was glossy and thick and smelled like ink.

"Nice book," I said.

"Should be for what Mildred Blueberg paid for it. She's the author. Went with one of those vanity presses. Poor thing had to purchase a ton. They still take up the whole garage at her lake house in Landover, and she self-published that thing ten years ago. I heard her family has to spend the good part of a day moving those boxes around just so they can get their boat out at the start of summer."

"How do they survive?" I asked, not really caring about the problems of the rich. I thumbed through the pages of the old photos from the early 1900s when Landover and Potter Grove were just being developed. The houses and buildings were all labeled alphabetically with a description of each along with their now photos.

Of course, Gate House looked the same, down to the bushes.

I sat down at the stool by Rosalie's turquoise-painted metal desk that was stacked full of papers, books, and half-finished paintings, and took my cute boots off, allowing my feet time off for good behavior.

Rosalie looked over my shoulder. "Mildred went around and took most of those 'now' photos herself, interviewing folks, and jotting down the stories they told her. And she's not a young woman," she added, like I thought a woman named Mildred might be.

Why hadn't I been interviewed?

I went straight to the bed and breakfast page next even though I wanted to look at the write-up and pictures of Gate House more. I'd look later.

I'd only seen the b&b in an occasional postcard at the Shop-Quik or when I'd pass it on my way to the university every once in a while whenever I had time to go the scenic route in college.

Jackson never wanted to stay there. "Staycations are for people too poor to go on real vacations," he'd say. "And, Gate House is much nicer than that awful bed and breakfast. There's no reason to stay at someplace subpar."

I never understood how in the world Jackson thought Gate House was much nicer until I saw the "then" photo of the bed and breakfast in Mildred's book. The b&b was also a Victorian, but it had originally been painted a dark color with bright contrasting trim, probably intended to look like a fun "gingerbread" kind of house. But the reality was a little more grim. A huge clown-like mouth seemed to form among the flourishes and swirls, complete with dead eyes and an imagined murmur in the background that said, "Good children get free lollipops..."

The after photo was a little better, only because the owner had painted it a consistent butter-nut yellow. It still looked like it was offering up stranger-danger candy, though.

In its heyday, the Landover Bed and Breakfast was the epitome of high society in Landover County. Built in 1877, it was originally owned by the Hind family, a family best known for the popular nineteenth-century treat Hind's Canned Yams. The family went into unexpected turmoil following the suicide of their oldest daughter, women's rights leader Bessilyn Hind.

Ms. Hind shot herself in the heart in 1906 during her 35th birthday celebration over a break-up with Sir Walter Timbre. The house was sold the following year, eventually becoming a bed and breakfast in 2002.

The Landover Bed and Breakfast is believed to be haunted by the suffragette's ghost with many saying they can hear Bessilyn roaming the halls calling out for Walty.

"They certainly make me out to be desperate and sad, don't they?"

I didn't even jump when I heard her behind me, reading over my shoulder. I was getting way too used to ghosts nowadays. I mouthed to Rosalie. "She's here."

Rosalie turned away, pretending to be interested in the stack of old paranormal books on her desk, probably trying to find some sort of all-important article on the detriments of channeling. The little hand on the EMF reader was going crazy, though.

Bessie turned to me. "As soon as you figure out who murdered me, I want you to write to the author of this book. I'm sure she will want to correct the bed and breakfast's chapter."

"I'm sure," I said. "Because Mildred Blueberg didn't spend enough on these. She's probably dead now anyway. This was published ten years ago."

"No, she's alive," Rosalie chimed in then looked down at her EMF reader. "Sorry to interrupt."

The suffragette didn't hear me, anyway. "Tell Mildred Blueberg I did not shoot myself in the heart. And I most certainly do not walk the halls of Landover Bed and Breakfast, pining for Walter, yelling out the name 'Walty,' of all things. For heaven's sake. I led the suffrage movement here in Landover. I wrote literature on it, made sure every man, woman, and child knew. I braved the winter in ridiculous dresses and tiny narrow boots designed by men to be prim and proper and stifling."

I thought about my own narrow boots I'd just taken off. Now, women stifled themselves, for a savings.

She went on. "Horribly stifling. Corsets so tight, if we coughed or laughed, we fainted. They were large and cumbersome and we had a hard time marching, but we did it. Time and time again. And I tell you one thing, I did not do it so I could have my death listed like that. I should have a better reputation than that drivel." Her voice rose at the end like a drill sergeant.

"I will try. But I can't make any guarantees."

Why did everyone want guarantees from their mediums nowadays?

"If we get a customer..." Rosalie finally said after a full minute of pretending not to notice me having a conversation with air. "Just maybe refrain from talking to anyone, you know, not really here."

I pointed my finger at Bessie. "Don't ride with me anymore," I said, even though it was my own fault for talking to a ghost in public.

Someone coughed behind us. I turned my head. It was Justin Fortworth. The deputy of Potter Grove, and my ex-boyfriend.

He looked me up and down, his dark eyes scanning the room as he held in a smile. "Who were you talking to just then?" he asked. "And do you always come to work in socked feet?"

Justin Fortworth drove me crazy the way he always seemed to sneak up on people without even trying. He ran a hand through his thick, dark hair as he waited for me to answer. The sleeves of his uniform were rolled along the curves of his upper arms, revealing the tattoos that also drove me crazy, in a different way.

"What's going on, officer?" I asked, ignoring his questions about the socked feet and the ghost I had been talking to.

Sheriff Caleb Bowman came up behind him. Caleb was Jackson's cousin, a lanky man with a sunken face and a bushy goatee that was about three shades darker than the men on the beard-dye commercials.

"The whole police force is here at once," Rosalie said hardly looking over. "This must be serious."

Caleb flipped open his notebook. "It's not. Just crazy Delilah Scott again. Did either of you see or hear anything weird today?"

Rosalie and I both looked at each other. "Define weird," she said.

Caleb scratched at his goatee. "Delilah Scott is sure something was stalking her while she was gardening this morning, about two hours ago. She told Christine she got the feeling she was being watched by something evil. Her words." He chuckled.

I got the feeling from the chuckle and the smirk on Caleb's face that he didn't believe her words. Delilah Scott was one of the oldest residents in Potter Grove who was still very active at the women's club because her mind was as sharp as a 30-year-old's.

The woman also lived in one of my favorite houses in Potter Grove, a storybook cottage just down the street from the Purple Pony, which was probably why the police were continuing their report over here. I didn't really know Delilah, though, except that she spent most of her time on safari or touring Europe, hiring guides to take her around.

She was also a Donovan, one of the founding families of Potter Grove.

Caleb continued. "I tried to tell Christine that Delilah was batty, but she insisted we come out here and make a report. Christine's just playing up to her mother-in-law again." Christine ran dispatch for the police department. Her mother-in-law was a member of the women's club, same as Delilah.

Caleb shook his head. "And all this because Delilah Scott said she heard something growling and rustling through her trees."

"Probably nothing," Justin interrupted. "We checked, but we didn't see anything unusual."

The whole incident made me remember a similar one two months earlier, though. I'd heard a strange growling, too, in the alley behind the Starlight Lounge. I told Justin about it at the time. I wondered if he remembered.

I opened my mouth to mention the incident, but he raised an eyebrow at me, making me stutter over my words and stop.

"Call me if you see or hear anything suspicious," Justin said, handing me his card, like I wouldn't know how to contact the police department in my city. Our hands touched for a second when I reached for it, and a jolt of electricity rushed up my arm, making me wonder why we broke up in the first place. I shook it off.

I knew from the recent channeling I'd done with Jackson that the way you remembered something in life wasn't always the way it went down in real time. We tended to put negative or positive spins on our fuzzy memories. And right now, I was only remembering the good times with this man, probably because Justin Fortworth was gorgeous and I hadn't technically had sex in years, unless you counted Mrs. Bellman's son, who I regretfully let my mother set me up with last year in a moment of weakness. I didn't count him, figuring my official sex count should only include men who didn't ask me to sneak out before their mothers woke up in the morning.

"Keep your eyes open," Justin said on his way to the door. He stared at me a little longer than I thought he would and I looked away, reminding myself there was no way I was going out with Justin Fortworth again. Not after the way things ended almost twelve years ago when I broke up with him to be with Jackson. He'd told everybody it was because I was a gold digger.

As they were leaving, Bessie appeared by my side again. "He's your Walter, huh?" she said, motioning toward the deputy who was looking back at me.

"If that means one of the jerks in your life you regret dating, then yes," I said. She was right, though. Justin was the kind of man I wouldn't want anyone thinking I cared enough about to walk the halls, calling out his name.

"We need a plan to prove Bessie's presence at the bed and breakfast," Rosalie said when the officers left.

"She'll come with us" I replied, gesturing to where the ghost was still hovering. "What better plan than the truth?"

CHAPTER 3

DREADFUL

*T*he bed and breakfast smelled like fresh roasted chestnuts when Rosalie and I stepped into the lobby after work around 7:00. Several comfy red floral couches were positioned strategically around the main fireplace with a crackling fire already going, even though it was warm for an evening in September. Large watercolor paintings hung on all the walls, some of random dogs being washed in metal tubs and others of garden parties with Victorian women in long dresses made from ridiculous amounts of fabric.

Rosalie motioned toward a large museum-quality display case at the back of the room with a sign above it labeled Bessilyn Hind. It held a headless mannequin wearing a faded champagne-colored gown, exactly like the one Bessilyn's ghost wore.

I stared at it a second; it seemed all too real now. Here was the exact gown, in the exact place she wore it. It still had beige splatter on it that I assumed was one-hundred-year-old blood along with what looked like gunpowder residue.

As if that wasn't enough, on the pedestal at the foot of her gown, was a gun with a sign that read. *A Gift to Regret: James Hind gave his daughter this gun in 1906 after she received death threats related to the suffrage movement.*

To the left of the gown was another pedestal. This one held a single glove. *Found on the side of the house during the chaos surrounding Bessilyn's untimely death. This driving glove was believed to have belonged to one of the distraught guests.*

The glove was floppy and huge, not like the ones Bessilyn wore as a ghost. A tan color with grease along the tips of its fingers. On the back wall, behind the display were two blown-up, grainy, black and white photos. One was of the glove on a rock next to a champagne glass. The other was Bessie with what I guessed was her family.

Bessilyn's eyes looked swollen and she was barely smiling in her party dress next to her sister, mother, and father. She was also very modestly dressed. The rest of her family dripped in jewels and broad smiles.

"Does anyone else think this is a little gruesome and tacky," I whispered under my breath to Rosalie.

"I've been in this bed and breakfast a lot, and I don't remember this," she said back.

"It's new. Got it a couple days ago," a booming voice said from across the room. I turned, almost jumping. A squatty woman in her forties with short, spiky, platinum-blonde hair and a pale complexion stood in front of the check-in counter near the front door. "Paula Henkel," she said, extending an arm and racing across the room with it. I shook her hand as soon as it got to me.

"Carly Taylor," I replied.

"Oh, I know all about you," her voice was gruff and confident. She looked me over like I was a car she might want to buy. "So you're the medium with the special powers?"

I shook my head. "Nope. I can see and talk to ghosts, but I don't have powers over them or anything. No power to see the future, read minds, or make things appear out of nowhere.

Sorry." It had become a pat answer now. I was getting asked about powers a lot lately.

She nodded slowly while her eyes still scanned me. I wasn't sure she heard a word I'd said. "Rosalie probably told you about the seance."

"Yes. I hear you want us to confirm your ghost is Bessilyn Hind before we agree to anything."

"Before *I* agree to anything," she corrected me.

I pointed to the display case with Bessilyn's dress. "I see you're a huge fan of hers."

"I'm a huge fan of money," she said. "Let's get that straight. I'm pretty skeptical about the rest of this malarkey, all the ghost stuff. But Bessie Hind is a name. And I'm selling dark history and death here. People stay at my bed and breakfast for a chance to see a historical ghost roaming the halls." She looked around her living room like the woman might be roaming right now. "I've spent a lot of money restoring this house to its original state, for the most part."

I nodded. I could see why "for the most part" didn't include the old scary paint job on the exterior.

She went on. "You're the most credible medium in the county, or so I hear. Can you do whatever mystical mumbo-jumbo you people do, and confirm Bessie's presence so we can move forward with the seance?"

I tried to tell her that wasn't how things worked. Ghosts came and went as they pleased. She put her hand up. "Just do it, or don't do it. But I haven't got time for excuses. My time is money, so if you can't do this seance, I'll find someone else who can."

I had no idea what kind of mystical mumbo-jumbo she was expecting, but I tried to look the part. A hundred bucks a piece was still a hundred bucks.

I walked around and looked longingly at the ceiling, taking deep breaths, trying to look like I was feeling the energy of the room.

I did feel an energy around me, but I was pretty sure it wasn't Bessie's. It seemed male to me. Less historical.

"Yes," I said. "Bessie's here."

"Did you talk to her just now in your mind?"

"No. We talk like normal people. With out-loud conversations and arguments and everything. She's here, but she doesn't want to talk right now."

I hadn't felt her at all. I only lied because I knew she'd be here. It was her idea to get Paula Henkel to seek me out in the first place.

"How does she like the new display?"

"She didn't say."

"Well, ask her."

"I'm sorry, but confirming is all I can do," I said, just as snippy as she'd been. "My time and my talent come at a price. I'm a huge fan of money too."

Rosalie elbowed me until I looked over. She gave me a thumbs-up and we signed the paperwork. The seance was officially on for a week from Saturday.

CHAPTER 4

DARK HISTORY

"*I* need your help," I announced the next afternoon to the short woman with coke-bottle glasses, sitting behind the main counter of the library. A cloud of white hair peeked around her huge, yellowing computer monitor.

"What do you need this time?"

"Town history," I said.

"Follow me." Mrs. Nebitt hopped off her stool and hustled over to the microfilm section. She was a squatty woman in a pair of green pants and a stretched-out, beige sweater that did nothing for her figure except create weird lumps where there probably weren't any.

Because the library was very small, the microfilm section was just a set of three metal cabinets in the periodicals area. And I was pretty sure one of those cabinets was empty. "Some day we're going to digitize our archives," she said, in a tone that suggested that was a radical idea. "Do you know what that means?"

I nodded even though I was tempted to hear her explanation.

She stopped in front of the gigantic computer on the desk in front of them. "Is this about Bessilyn Hind and the seance coming up next weekend at the bed and breakfast?"

I turned my head to the side. "How on earth did you know about that?"

"I received an invitation," she said with a grin, which made me realize the woman's face could make other expressions in addition to her usual scowl. "The new owner came over first thing this morning."

"That was nice of her," I said. I knew there were only a few spots at any given seance table for others, probably six, max, for this one.

"Yes." The older woman sat down and clicked on the keyboard in front of the research computer. "Apparently, I'm considered one of the most distinguished members in town. So I get my ticket for free."

"Ticket? So, she's charging people?"

"There's a dinner too. You and Rosalie have quite a draw with the older ladies at the country club. And Bessilyn Hind was also a member there. Oh here we are," she said, staring at the screen while she took out a tiny pencil and scratch paper from the plastic basket on the side of the desk. "Just Bessilyn?"

It took me a second to process what she was saying. My mind was still on the seance. "No, Sir Walter Timbre too, and Bessie's parents..." I looked at my notes app. "Greta and James Hind. Her sister and brother-in-law. Pleasant and Troy Brillows."

"One at a time, please," she said, scribbling down names onto the scratch paper.

"So, how much is she charging for the dinner and the seance?" I asked, suddenly much more interested in making sure Rosalie and I were getting our fair share.

"There's a flier on the front counter." Mrs. Nebitt pointed toward a bright pink piece of paper propped up in a plastic display case on the main counter next to the check out. "I'm selling tickets for her."

I rushed across the room, my hands shaking so much I could barely pull my phone out of my purse. I clenched my teeth as I clicked a couple photos of it.

Meet the Ghost of
Landover's Bed and Breakfast
The Landover Bed and Breakfast presents...
The Conjuring of a Suicidal Suffragette with Carly Taylor and
Rosalie Cooper
$50 per ticket for the 9:00 seance show
Cocktail hour and Buffet-style dinner
also available at 5:30

It went on to talk about Bessilyn and her suicide, the new historical display cases, my fame as Jackson Bowman's ex who inherited Gate House and was briefly tangled in the stripper murders.

I texted the photos to Rosalie then stormed back over to the periodicals section where Mrs. Nebitt waited for me, tapping her pencil.

As soon as I returned, she scooted to the edge of her seat, pushing the film into place and twisting the knob on the side until she stopped on an article. Sir Walter's obituary.

Sir Walter Charles Timbre, heir to Crown Frozen Vegetables, died just before his 76th birthday on October 9, 1942 after a long bout with cancer. He is survived by his wife of 35 years Katharine Timbre, famous in her own right for her role in the women's suffrage movement; their two children, Byron and Walter Jr; and five grandchildren.

"Welp, he didn't wait long," I remarked to Mrs. Nebitt who was still sitting by my side "helping" me with the microfilm. We both knew I only needed help getting things set up. She blinked her humungous-looking eyes at me.

I pointed toward the screen. "It says his wife of 35 years," I explained. "He must've married this Katharine woman in 1907. Yet in 1906, he was still engaged to Bessilyn Hind. I wonder if she was the reason they broke up. I also noticed he had a thing for women's rights leaders." The article included a photo of Sir Walter. My mouth fell open. Broad shoulders, full beard and mustache that wasn't waxed or weird, and soft vulnerable eyes. The photo was not of a 76-year-old Sir Walter.

"He was very handsome," Mrs. Nebitt said, pointing out the obvious.

We both stared at him a second before looking up some of the other articles on her scratch piece of paper. Bessie's parents died six months after she did, in a car accident. Her sister, Pleasant, died in 1950 from "natural causes." And Pleasant's husband passed on in 1926.

"Pleasant Brillows. That's a name I haven't heard in a very long time. She used to go to First Methodist when I was a little girl," she said, matter-of-factly, making me just about fall over onto the microfilm machine. I'd forgotten this woman was basically a walking history book herself, born and raised in Landover. "You knew Pleasant?"

She nodded. "Only she wasn't very pleasant."

I somehow refrained from making a "pot calling the kettle black" comment right then.

The older lady leaned back in her rickety wooden chair. It squeaked under her weight. "I remember her from church. This was the early 1940s. I was a child so my memory is a little unreliable, but I know she was very scary to children. She always wore black and never smiled. It was one of my first memories, actually. I had to sit next to her one time. Mrs. Brillows opened a butter-scotch candy in front of me. I was mesmerized by her hands, how they shook as she opened the candy, how pale they were with large blue veins running down the length of them. I was terrified, but mesmerized. She had a whole bag of candies by her side, and

I was a child, so I smiled and motioned toward the bag. She nodded approvingly."

"That was pleasant," I said.

"When I reached for one, she swatted my hand so hard it left a pink mark. My mother never made me sit by her again."

I chuckled. "Whatever happened to her?" I asked.

"She eventually left the church, so I'm not sure. I heard she died penniless. Canned yams stopped selling like they used to, I suppose. Serves her right."

I stared at the screen full of names and dates. It was weird how time changed everything. From how our hands looked to what we ate as a society. And how each life was eventually just a snippet, like a faded article on microfilm, a tiny part of a much broader story.

The library suddenly seemed extra quiet to me. Lonely. The clock ticked away on a nearby wall.

"You know who would be an excellent reference for all of this? My friend Mildred. She wrote a book on Landover a few years back."

I snatched my phone from my purse once again before Mrs. Nebitt could change her mind. "Mildred Blueberg? I would love to talk to her. Do you have her number?"

Mrs. Nebitt swatted the air. "Why on earth would I have my address book with me here at work? I'll look it up for you later." She glanced at my phone. The screen was still on the photo I'd taken of the flier.

"The seance is more than a hundred dollars per ticket if you include dinner." She lowered her voice. "But I guess we both get in for free. Lucky us."

"Yes, lucky us," I repeated. I couldn't wait for Rosalie to see just how lucky we were to have signed that contract.

CHAPTER 5

COOLER HEADS

*C*artoon flames bolted from Rosalie's ears when I stumbled under the unicorn that afternoon.

"Why in the hell are we only getting a hundred dollars each to do this seance if she's selling tickets for fifty dollars a pop?" Rosalie said, her face beet red. "And that's not including dinner and cocktail hour. Cocktail hour. Honestly. So we're nothing but the entertainment."

I shrugged. "I guess there's not much we can do about it now."

Rosalie didn't hear me. "Buffet-style dinners are what they serve when they expect a hell of a lot of people. Isn't that right?" Rosalie only cussed when she was upset. She'd said *hell* five times in the two minutes I'd been there; I was counting. "They're the potlucks of fancy dining, huh?"

She flipped through the pages of the contract we'd signed with Paula while pacing the room. The limp she usually had from her bad hip was barely noticeable. "Nowhere does it say in this damn paperwork that she would be selling tickets at all."

"I guess we should have specified how many people could show up."

"The hell we should have," she said, picking up her cell phone. "This is not our fault. She was purposely deceptive. I do see something in this contract that we can still use, though. This 24-hour cancellation clause. I bet she put that in for herself." A calmness fell over her face as she left a message on Paula's voicemail. I was pretty sure Paula was not going to be nearly as calm when she heard it.

~

BESSIE AND JACKSON were arguing in the living room when I got home a little before 7:00. Rex greeted me by begging for the dinner I was late in getting him. I put his meal in the microwave then listened in on the argument in the next room.

"Stop being so sadistic," Jackson said. "You used to be living. Is it too much to remember what that was like and be concerned for her psyche?"

"There could be an important clue there."

"But those clues won't involve the exact second of... impact. Be reasonable."

"Reasonable? I'm not the one being unreasonable."

"Except that you are."

"I have an idea probably no man has ever thought of," Bessie said, turning to me. "Why don't we let her decide?"

I knew what they were talking about. It was what I'd been the most worried about too. The final moment. The gunshot part. Channelings were just like living the memory out in real life. I would be feeling death, for the first time.

The microwave beeped and I turned back toward the kitchen, my boots digging into my feet like a constant reminder of just how humanly fragile I was. I felt pain. Every bit of it.

"I can handle it," I said, even though I wasn't sure. "And Bessie's right. There could be a clue at that moment."

Bessie threw Jackson a smug smile. It gleamed in the darkness. "Tell me, dear. Did you find anything interesting in your research today?" she asked.

I wondered how much of my research I should tell the apparition or how much she already knew. Was it okay to tell her that her parents died shortly after she had, or that her sister had grown into a mean old woman who smacked little kids' hands after offering them candy? It was strange because I was privy to stuff she probably had no idea about.

"Nothing worth talking about," I said. "Are you ready?"

"I was murdered ready," she said, chuckling at her joke.

I sat down on one of my dining room chairs and took off my boots to get comfortable. My heart raced for no reason, and I told myself to calm down, but all I could hear was the clock ticking away in the background again. I heard a lot of clocks lately, not sure why.

I blinked into the dimness of my dining room. It wasn't too late to back out. I could still say, "no." Problem was, I was feeling drawn to the channelings. I'd been looking forward to this all day. So, why was I suddenly feeling weird about it?

Bessie looked human, aside from her glow, and the fact she was hovering just above the hardwood floor in front of me.

She seemed to sense my apprehension. "Just keep your eyes closed until I tell you. Breathe deeply and try to make your mind open and free of thoughts."

I took one deep breath after another. Inhale, exhale. Like Jackson had done when I channeled with him, she waited until my heart was steady and my breathing calm.

I smelled her first. Just before she entered. The faintest smell of mint tea, which was odd and unexpected. She was softer than Jackson had been the first time I'd done this, more encompassing. A powerful ghost must have an easier touch.

"Do you hear me?' she asked, her voice echoed inside my mind.

"Yes," I replied. I took a deep breath, which seemed to echo off my rib cage like Darth Vader.

"You'll get used to it," I told myself. "Just like last time."

"Yes," she said. "You will."

Whether I was comfortable with this invasion of my body or not, we were one. And it was happening. It was now too late to back out. I breathed in again, my loud exhale morphing into the sound of lively piano music, mostly the playful, repetitive cords you hear before a piece begins.

A man's voice bellowed over them in a vocal warming exercise. "Me. Me. Me… Usually, I get paid to dance," he yelled. Lots of applause and laughter followed. I could tell, even with my eyes closed, that the crowd was pretty substantial. The man continued. "Please, maestro. My key." The piano played. "I said my key…" The man repeated in a falsetto high-pitched voice. More laughter.

"You can open your eyes now," Bessilyn told me.

Blinking around the darkened room, I could hardly believe it. The house didn't look at all creepy on the inside like it had in the photos I saw in *Landover County: Then and Now*.

A small orchestra sat off to my right where a man stood in front of a piano, singing like he was straight out of an old record.

To my left, three large tables, each beautifully trimmed in gold and white linens, were pushed against the back wall to create a dance floor where about seven couples found places to dance.

One table had nothing but drinks and glasses. Another hors d'oeuvres. And the third, the makings of a feast. I smelled bread, and some sort of meat in what could have been a burgundy sauce. Many people sat at tables situated around the dance floor, eating and talking, watching the dancers.

My stomach growled. I'd forgotten to eat before the channeling, and I tried to get myself not to care, not to smell things. I had a job to do.

I realized I was cupping something in my gloved hand, and I

looked down to see a glass of champagne. Bessie took a sip as she shuffled her feet to the music. The champagne was extremely dry. The couples dancing around her all seemed to know the same dance moves, probably a waltz of some sort.

"Are all of these people your friends," I asked Bessie.

"Hardly any of them."

Someone tapped her shoulder and she turned around. A short, older man in his 80s. "May I have the honor?" he asked.

She warmed when she saw him. "Popsy. Of course."

He slipped his hand into Bessie's and they spun around the dance floor, in perfect time with the other dancers, round and round, smiling at the many guests seated around them. A large chandelier overhead glistened in the lamp lights accenting the staircase toward the back of the room. It was decadent, all right. And I suddenly felt like a star, like all eyes were on me, but not all of them were happy-for-you eyes. I mentally felt daggers.

He leaned in and whispered in Bessie's ear as we danced. "I heard you had to go before the judge on a matter of speeding again."

"Yes." She smiled.

"How fast were you going this time?"

"You would have been very proud."

"Someday you'll take this old man around, I hope." They twirled to the music as they talked. "I wanted to get you a car of your own for your birthday so you wouldn't have to scare the town in your father's. A faster one. Wouldn't that have been something?"

She smiled at him and squeezed his hand. "That would have been."

"Your father said you didn't have a need for it. A need? Who makes purchases because they have a need?"

Bessie looked down at her feet, almost losing her step as they danced.

His breath smelled like hard liquor as he yelled over the

music. "The world may be quick to tell you all the things you can't do in life. But remember, they're only right if you listen to them." He winked. "They told me, 'Jimmy, you'll never make money canning vegetables. People can can their own. They don't need you to do it.' I didn't listen, and not listening to them changed my life."

"So your advice is not to listen to advice?"

"Exactly," he said, kissing her cheek. "But then, you already knew that. Your father's the one I worry about. I shouldn't have pressured him to give up medicine and take over the business. He's far too logical for it." He paused, his brow furrowing. "I suppose logic has a place in business too, especially when business gets mixed with love and cooler heads need to prevail."

"It's all right, Popsy."

"No, it's not. I tell you when *Sir Walter* ended your engagement, I'd have ended our business partnership with that whole snobbish Timbre family right then and there if I were still in charge of the cannery."

"But Father did cut ties with the Timbres."

"He did?"

"Last week."

"It's no longer my business, I suppose."

The music stopped, and her grandfather hugged her and wished her a happy birthday. "I don't know how much more your grandmother can take tonight. Pleasant's got her watching the baby again. But if I don't get another chance to tell you, it was a lovely party, my dear. Would've been lovelier with a new car." He winked. "We'll go shopping for that as soon as you get back. You'll have a need for it then."

"Get back from where?"

"Oh dear. Forget I said anything."

"Popsy, it's too late."

He rushed off. In her head, she said to me, "My grandfather always did stuff like that, saying the wrong things. Probably where I got it from. My parents' birthday surprise was a trip to Europe that I didn't want, and didn't get to take."

"What was the business deal he was talking about that involved Sir Walter's family?" I asked.

She didn't answer me, quickly moving on. "Over here is my sister, Pleasant," she said as her gaze turned to a stunning brunette around 30. "And my grandmother."

Beside the woman I guessed was Pleasant was an older lady dressed in a severe black dress with a high, white collar. What looked like a baby sailor sat on her lap, a toddler in a bright blue and white sailor outfit who grabbed at the candles and mints sitting in the middle of the table. The older woman swatted the boy's hand from the candy dish when he reached across the table. At least now I knew how Pleasant had turned out the way she had later in life.

Pleasant looked just like she had in the photo in the display case at the bed and breakfast. Simple dress, with lots of jewelry.

"Pleasant, you look beautiful," Bessie said to her sister, grinding her teeth a little as she smiled. "And you brought Troy junior. Wonderful surprise."

"I brought them all," she replied, nervously tugging on an ear while motioning toward the two older children in the room. What looked like a five-year-old girl with blonde curls had a finger in one of the serving dishes at the dessert table. A boy of about seven yanked the girl's hair. "Mother said you wouldn't mind. She told me you love surprise guests."

"She said that?"

"Yes. She said you tried to invite some yourself."

Bessie bit her lip harder. "Only my friends from the club."

"Where are your suffragist friends anyway? Please point them out. I've been dying to meet them. Did Mother approve?"

Bessie shook her head, "no," but added a smile. "Mother's right, though. I do love surprise guests. A couple of them might sneak in later. I told them they should. It will liven things up a bit, don't you think?"

"If by liven things up, you mean father's temper. He'll be mad as hops," her sister replied, and they both laughed.

Bessie talked to me in her head. "Telling Pleasant she could bring her children was my mother's way of punishing me for trying to invite my friends."

"Sorry," I said.

A woman shrieked on the dance floor, and Bessie's attention went straight to Pleasant's older two kids, who were now playing what looked like a shoving game of tag around the dancers.

Pleasant motioned to them. "I really do hope you don't mind I brought the children. Mother said you wouldn't, but I wasn't sure."

"Mind? I wouldn't have it any other way. Your children are the sweetest ever. Just little bundles of life." The boy on her grandmother's lap picked his nose.

We kissed Pleasant's cheek then left.

"You couldn't tell your sister the truth?" I asked as soon as we'd moved on.

"She knew the truth. Who brings children to an adult party? She did it to show off. To show everyone there that she was married and I was not. To show that she had children..." She stopped herself. "It was silly, really. But I did care about that kind of stuff at the time."

I completely understood. The same thing went on with my family. I was 31 and there wasn't a conversation at my mother's house that didn't include questions about when I was going to marry again, because really, didn't I want children?

Bessie's voice trailed off a little as she spoke to me, remembering things. "And poor Pleasant didn't really have a choice but to bring her children. She didn't have a nanny. My father was quite controlling. And he told her, in no uncertain terms, that if she married Troy, he was limiting her funds. Girls of a certain status shouldn't marry service men."

I was taking all sorts of mental notes. Bessie's father decided a lot for his adult children. And her mother had unusual punishments.

She went on. "There's Troy senior, her awful husband, right now," she said, looking toward the bar where a tall thin man in military dark bell bottoms and a neckerchief was ordering a drink. "I don't really know him even though they've been married eight years now. He's Navy. Gone most the time, which I've heard is probably for the best."

Troy raised his glass to the bartender who nodded politely. His seven-year-old son ran by him, almost making him drop his glass and Troy yanked him hard by the back of the boy's sailor outfit, sending him to the floor, ending the children's shoving game. "Pleasant!" he yelled, looking all around. "Where is that woman?"

Pleasant rushed over, toddler kicking at her side. "Yes, dear."

"Take care of your children." He directed his bloodshot eyes to Pleasant's grandparents, who were heading out the door with their coats in hand. Her grandmother looked down, suddenly very interested in the buttons on her dress seam.

"He'd been trying to get my grandparents to pay for a nanny for ages," Bessie explained to me. "It's a bit of a family joke that he lets his children run wild at family functions on purpose to try to persuade them."

Pleasant scowled at her older son, his nose bleeding from the fall. Someone handed her a cloth napkin and she dabbed at the blood while holding tightly to her toddler.

Bessie headed out the back of the party toward the other side of the house.

"You didn't want to help your sister?" I asked.

"I wouldn't know how." She laughed. "I'm not much with children. I'm sure one of the housekeepers helped, although they avoided her children as much as I did."

At the back of the room, past the area that now housed the front counter of the bed and breakfast, were a set of doors that seemed like they led to a back porch.

"The garden room," she said as she clung to the wall, approaching it slowly. "This is where my father's outcast friends always spent their time at a party, probably so they wouldn't have to worry about trivial things like manners."

We stayed in the shadows as we peeked into the room, which was as large as my mother's backyard in Indianapolis. It was surrounded by windows on all sides, the light of the lamps reflecting off of them, giving each person sitting around the nearby patio table a sinister glow. There were about ten of them, equally split between men and women.

The room itself was filled with wrought iron patio furniture and extra large art.

"I'm sure you'll recognize one," she said to me at the same moment I spotted him. A thick man who resembled Teddy Roosevelt with his vest and round glasses. Henry Bowman. He was taking off a clunky pair of gloves that looked just like the one in the display case.

CHAPTER 6

DRIVING FORCES

"*A*nd that's all there is to driving, or that's what they told me at the dealership," he said, tossing his gloves onto the table, almost knocking over a couple of glasses. "Who wants to go for a spin?"

"Not now, Henry," the thick blonde woman next to him said. I knew from the photos around Gate House, she was Marjorie Bowman, Jackson's great grandmother. It was funny how I thought she looked grandmotherly and sweet in her photos. In person, she seemed more like a prison guard.

Bessilyn whispered to me in her head, even though there was zero chance anyone could hear her. "You couldn't go to a party without people bragging about their cars anymore. The newer and more expensive, the more important you were."

"Not much has changed," I said.

The group of guests sitting at the informal table in front of us were an older group, most in their 40s and 50s, who all seemed too drunk to know they were laughing and toasting to nothing, which was probably why they hadn't noticed Bessie standing at the door. I checked their faces, but didn't see anyone who looked like Eliza.

"This party. It's just unseemly, that's all," one woman said, her wine glass spilling as she leaned over. "If you ask me, the Hinds indulge their 35-year-old child far too much."

The table roared with laughter. Several people toasted.

"I have to admit, she does look good for her age. There is something to be said for the figure of a childless woman," Henry added, adjusting his Theodore-Roosevelt-looking spectacles. He outlined the shape of an hourglass in the air with his fingertips then turned to the men at the table for confirmation. They all looked down at their cufflinks.

Marjorie dutifully stepped in. "That's only when comparing her to her sister tonight, who's apparently given up on fashion anymore. Did you see Pleasant's awful frock?"

The other ladies laughed knowingly.

"Motherhood changes women, and not for the better," Henry said. He turned to his wife. "Present company excluded..." No one said a thing, so Henry continued, like he was trying to correct his gaffe. "And perhaps you all are right. A woman of Bessilyn's age should probably prefer a ladies garden party to celebrate her birthday. Something more suitable for her situation."

"A party of equally aging spinsters? Henry, that might be hard to come by." Marjorie said, touching his arm. The table burst out with laughter again.

Bessie's voice was calm for a woman hearing such insults about herself. "I'd introduce you to Jackson's great grandparents, but this is when I left them that night. You can imagine why."

"But," I said, hesitating to go anywhere. "Eliza's not here. You said she was."

"Yes, she is. Look in the shadows. It was an odd arrangement the Bowmans had with their nanny, or house nurse. I never knew what she was. She didn't sit with them. They barely acknowledged each other."

Henry pulled a deck of cards out of his jacket pocket and

shuffled them. "I learned this trick in Australia on one of my business trips."

"He's such a good businessman," Marjorie said, looking up at her husband with doting eyes.

On his other side, in a chair like she was banished to the darkness of the corner, sat a woman who looked just like me. She had a single lamp next to her on a small table, but even in the dimness of the light I could tell for certain it was her, same blondish brown curls, same eyes. She didn't look up or engage with the rest of the table. She appeared to be knitting and mumbling to herself.

"What did you say your business was, Henry?" one of the men asked.

"I didn't. Now, pick a card," he announced to the table, spreading the deck out face down along his fingertips. A woman with long gloves indulged him.

"I thought there'd be more yams than this," Henry chuckled, his tight vest practically bursting at the seams as he moved the cards around to shuffle them. "I heard this aging spinster's party was built on them."

We turned and left, back down the hall to the main part of the house, passing a beautiful bust of George Washington on the way by and some old paintings of Bessie's relatives that seemed to watch your every move. The orchestra had picked up to a lively song I actually recognized. "Give My Regards to Broadway."

"Are you okay?" I asked Bessie.

"Yes. I was used to being the joke at this point," she half chuckled. "I chose not to marry, so I am naturally labeled a spinster. It's disturbing how easily it flows off the tongue, though, as if labeling a 'cat' a 'cat.' Walter was five years my senior, a man already forty, but he was still considered a young, eligible bachelor ripe for family. No one was surprised when he broke up with the spinster woman too old to give him the life he deserved. No one but me, I suppose."

She looked down as she walked back out to the party. "Chin up. Let's go meet my parents. I should warn you, though." She paused at a beautifully adorned table trimmed in golden flowers. "Let's just say, it's been a while since they've been happy with me. I should also tell you, I suspect them in my... untimely demise."

We approached what could only have been the most prominent table at the party with a view that was front and center of the dance floor and the orchestra. Men in tailored suits with pocket squares and vests; women in feathered hats with diamonds and pearls, hair all in neatly swept up-dos. Bessie kissed an older couple each on the cheek.

"My parents," she told me.

Her mother looked much younger than her father, a thin woman with dark hair and blue eyes. Her father was bald with a gray mustache.

"Are you enjoying the party you requested?" her father asked.

"Stop, James," her mother quipped. "Don't listen to him," she explained to the rest of the table. "I insisted on the party. Bessie didn't even want anything so extravagant. She's the family humanitarian, mind you. But, I insisted. If we're going to have a party, we should do it right. Bring up the spirits around here."

Everyone nodded. They all knew what spirits needed lifting, Bessie's engagement ending and all.

"Don't just stand there, my dear," a plump woman with glasses said to Bessie, motioning to the chair next to her.

"My mother's best friend, Doris," Bessie explained to me as we sat next to her. Bessie fidgeted with her hands, looking down at her gloves.

"I didn't get a chance to say happy birthday," the woman said. "Let me get a look at you."

Bessie looked up into the woman's pale green eyes.

"Beautiful. You're still so beautiful. You'll find someone. Don't wait too long, though."

Bessie squeezed her hands into tiny little fists under the table. Her mother shot her a look.

"Thank you, Mrs. Smalls," Bessie said, dutifully.

"We were just talking about you."

"No," the man beside her said. "We were just talking about my new Moon motor car. It's a beaut. You should see it. Cold steel and four cylinders. Only three thousand dollars."

"Herbert, stop bragging. He's going to kill himself with that."

"Now I know why she tells me to drive it all the time," he said, and the rest of the table laughed.

"No, but it's why I won't let him teach me," she added to more laughter.

"You could learn to drive it, too," Bessie said. "I could teach you at the women's club. You won't die."

Everyone stared at her and I could feel Bessie's cheeks growing warmer as she thought things through. "It's quite simple. Only a few things to master, really."

"Bessilyn's been very busy at the orphanage as well," her mother said quickly. "Tell us about your work with the orphans."

"I never knew what to say at times like this," Bessie told me. "My mother's idea of me and my idea of myself never went hand and hand."

Bessilyn leaned into Doris. "I've been very busy with the woman's suffrage movement too. I think having the right to vote will help other causes…"

Her father cut her off. "That's enough, Bessilyn. We talked about this."

Bessie threw her hands on her hips. "I'm sorry, Father," she said, her voice rising in intensity that didn't at all sound remorseful. She swallowed and continued, looking up at the table now, a new-found confidence in her throat. "I'd forgotten it's perfectly fine for men to talk about everything from the cost of their new automobiles to the hour glass figure of a woman, but God forbid a woman should bring up the fact that she might like to have the right to vote because that topic is going far too far."

"It's fine for you to have your ideas. But don't force them on our guests." Her father wiped his glasses with his napkin. "Please forgive our daughter. She seems to have forgotten what polite conversation is."

"No, it's perfectly all right," Doris said. "Herbert and I feel just as strongly. Don't we, darling? Only, we're members of the Anti-Women's Suffrage Movement."

Bessie's face dropped. "But you're a woman."

"Glad you noticed, dear. There are very large differences between men and women in society, and not just our looks. That's precisely why I'm a member. I believe that in order for things to run properly in a society, we must never forget our places." She turned to Bessie's mother. "Isn't that right, Greta?"

Bessie's mother, Greta, threw a hand over her mouth, shooting Bessie a horrified look for dragging her into such a conversation. "I... I," she said, taking a deep breath. She took a long sip of her wine and composed herself. "I, for one, would hate to mess with all the meetings and boring literature that casting a considerate vote would entail," she said, smiling nervously into her glass.

The other women nodded at the table.

"Then skip it," Bessie replied. "You don't have to vote. But to deny the rest of us that right because you can't bother to educate yourself is reprehensible at best and pathetic kowtowing to your male counterparts over here at worst."

An audible gasp fell over the table.

"Bessilyn Hind," her father yelled. "If this rudeness is what we have to look forward to with the women's movement then no wonder it's failing."

"It's not failing," Bessie began then stopped herself when she looked around the table at the older faces who all seemed dumbstruck by her boldness. "You wish it were failing, but wishing won't make it so. And that's what scares you all the most."

The woman Bessie had been talking to could not seem to take her eyes off her lap. "I hear you're going on a trip, Bessie. That sounds lovely." She pretended to lower her voice so only her husband would hear. "I can see why they're sending you off."

Bessie's eyebrows scrunched. "A trip?"

"It was a surprise, Doris," Bessie's father said, standing up and reaching into the pocket of his dark suit jacket. "I was going to make an announcement, but now that the cat's out of the bag…"

He waved an envelope in the air as he addressed the table. "Not exactly perfect timing, but then I'm starting to believe perfect timing doesn't exist in life. At least not in mine."

The table awkwardly chuckled.

"Happy birthday, my dear. Your present." He handed Bessilyn the envelope, and I couldn't take my eyes off of him. His smug smile, the curve of his chin, there was something very familiar about the man. But how on earth could there be anything familiar about a man from 1906?

Bessie opened the envelope while talking to me. "Their table already knew what I was getting. My parents were tired of their embarrassing daughter living close enough to their friends that they couldn't lie about her."

She pulled the ticket out and held it up for the table to see. "A ticket to Europe."

"An all-expense-paid trip," her mother chimed in. "She'll be traveling all around Europe for a bit. Great Britain, Ireland, Germany… So this will be farewell for a while for our dear Bessie, I'm afraid. But don't feel sorry for her. Oh no. She's about to have the time of her life. Her uncle Frederick in London has even offered her a job at his dress shop, so if it works out, Bessie may want to stay."

Bessie dutifully walked over to her father and kissed him on the cheek then did the same for her mother, her eyes welling up into tears as she thanked them.

"The poor girl's choked up," Doris said.

Bessie could barely get her mouth to form words. "Thank you, really. I'm so grateful, but I can't. Not now. I'm in charge of the meetings at my women's club. I have one coming up this month."

"Not anymore, you don't," her father replied. "And you're welcome. Enough said."

The people at the table all seemed happy for her. Voices rose over the music. "Europe? What a splendid idea."

"Maybe she'll find a husband of an exotic nature. That's what my cousin did. And she was almost as old as Bessilyn."

"I heard from Henry Bowman that Australia's beautiful. You should go there too."

Bessie smiled at each guest before excusing herself. She was holding in tears when she left.

Bessie's voice was loud and quick through the channeling, though. "They didn't know how to answer questions about me anymore. That's why they were sending me off. That's what hurt the most. They were tired of the jokes around town. The awful, threatening letters to the suffragist movement, and the hard glances during dinner conversations. It would've been better for them if I committed suicide. I see that now."

"What are you saying? Being sent to Europe and being murdered are two very different things," I reminded her. "We'll figure it out, but it might not have been your parents."

"A suicide wouldn't cost them a dime."

"Except a daughter."

"Pleasant's the daughter they always wanted. My friends from the women's club… My mother wouldn't even let me invite them to my party. She said they were a 'dowdy and sad lot'. I don't even like anyone here."

She looked down at her boots and rushed off through the crowd.

"And the worst part? I didn't even eat at my party. My corset had been too tight."

Damn it. My own stomach rumbled louder, realizing it wouldn't get to sample anything after all.

Then my focus turned to my waist. The thing wrapped around my middle suddenly seemed especially tight as it squeezed at my rib cage. Had there always been this dull ache along my diaphragm? I almost felt like I couldn't breathe properly now.

I'd really wanted to eat everything here. The pudding. The tiny sandwiches. Whatever it was in that burgundy sauce. I didn't even care if it was squirrel. I just wanted that sauce.

I also felt this incredible need to dance. Feel my feet tapping along the wooden planks of the dance floor while listening in on the people from 1906, see what they smelled like, talked about besides cars and hourglass figures. Maybe even flirt with one of the men milling about, pretending not to be smitten with Bessie.

We wouldn't be doing any of that now. "Focus, Carly. You're here for the clues," I reminded myself. I needed to be objective and aware. This was not about me.

Bessie crumpled the envelope in her fist and rushed across the dance floor, straight into the arms of one of those 1906 men I was just thinking about. I looked up to see the twinkling hazel eyes of a light-haired man in a suit with a perfectly trimmed mustache and beard. He was carrying a hat as he gently held my shoulders. Bessie's knees wobbled a little, and she didn't have time to think.

"Walty," she said. "What are you doing here?"

"So…," I said in my head as we continued staring at him. "You did call him Walty."

CHAPTER 7

NEVER LET THEM SEE YOU CARE

Sir Walter Timbre was gorgeous, all right, even better looking in person, tall with broad shoulders and a chiseled chin. And there was also something familiar about him too, just like with Bessilyn's father, but I couldn't place it.

Bessie's gaze went from the bow of Walter's lips to his eyes then back again. I could tell her heart was racing and she was sweating in the ridiculous get-up she had on.

She quickly got it together enough to give him an awkward, obligatory hug. He smelled like he'd just stepped out of a shower.

"I shouldn't have come," he said. His accent was British, something I should've expected given his title. But I was still surprised.

"No, it's fine. I just didn't know."

All eyes turned to us. People stopped mid-dance to look over and gawk. One woman dropped her plate. Bessie didn't seem to notice.

"I want to talk to you," he said, lowering his voice. "Alone."

"Go ahead. Talk."

"Not here. Everyone's staring."

Bessie's voice rose. "Of course they're staring, Walter. You broke up with me. They want to know why you're here. We all

45

want to know why." She turned to the stunned spectators standing around the dance floor with their mouths open. "Don't we?"

He grabbed a couple of champagne glasses from off a nearby tray and pulled Bessie outside. The chatters of gossip rose up in the house as soon as the door closed.

The night air was surprisingly warm, calming almost. Frogs croaked all around us. A horse whinnied and rustled in the front lawn where horse buggies and cars were lined up, festive lanterns surrounding the driveway, lighting the roped-off area.

He handed Bessie a glass and she took a long sip, champagne bubbles tickling her nose as she stared off at the parking lot, pretending she didn't want to be staring at Walter.

I tried to get Bessie to look at him, this gorgeous man who was probably trying to apologize and maybe even ask us to dance or something. She never looked up.

Walter cupped her chin in his hand and gently brought her face up to catch his gaze. For what seemed like a full minute, they just stared at each other, or he stared at Bessie, and Bessie tried not to look like she cared.

"I knew the second I ended our engagement that I'd made the biggest mistake of my life," he said. "I love you, Bessie."

"Do you?" Bessie's voice was curt. "Because it seems as if you only realized this last week, when my father broke up with you."

She rushed down the porch stairs and into the night, heart racing, fists clenched. I tried to stay calm and detached, concentrating on the way the wind blew softly along my neckline and the smells that went with it, mostly horse manure. Walty didn't immediately follow us and Bessie leaned against a large oak tree on the side of the house, her body wanting to take a large breath, her corset not allowing it.

There were a lot of clues and suspects. And I took a second to try to think things through. Bessie's parents were certainly suspicious. The poor girl had also been getting anti-suffragist death threats from someone who could easily have been her parents' friends. Or her parents.

"I was angry," Bessie said to me in her head, through the consciousness we now shared. "My parents told me all along Walter was only showing me interest in order to seal the deal on the business partnership. His family owned a frozen vegetable business not too far from my family's cannery. It was a perfect merger for both families, and they were suspicious."

"What do you think?"

"I didn't want to believe my parents, but they were right. Walter and I dated for six months, got engaged at about a year. Then, when they'd all agreed to the business, and it was too late to back out, he broke up with me." Her voice lowered. "But my parents got the last laugh. There was a little-known clause built into the contract for them to back out, and they used it. It's why he's here."

Footsteps crunching through sticks and grass grew louder as someone approached, and Bessie looked up, watching the shadowy silhouette of a man in a dark suit coat.

"Do you remember," Walter began when he reached her. He bent down to catch Bessie's attention, shooting her a smile. A strand of her hair had fallen free from its perfect placement in the up-do, and Walter swept it away with the light touch of his pinkie. "When I'd climb that horrible trellis to your window? You'd leave it half-unlatched just for me."

"Don't flatter yourself. I'm afraid the old window's always been that way. It wasn't installed correctly."

"You are a stubborn woman."

"You used to say my stubbornness was endearing. Of course that was before my parents made the deal with your family. As soon as that happened, your true colors came out."

He was pinching his hat now, almost grabbing at it. He took a deep breath, looked up at the dark sky then back down at Bessie. "When I told you we should end our engagement, and you didn't seem to care, I… I realized I did care. I do care. I love you. And I don't give a damn about business."

She didn't say a word.

He went on. "I let the opinions of others cloud my thoughts."

"What opinions?" Bessie's mind raced. "Your mother's?"

"I'm her only son. She wants to see me have children."

"And I'm too old for that." Bessie gripped the tree tighter, its rough bark digging into her fingernails, sending a little pain up along our hand.

"I don't give a damn about children either. I love you. Only you. I should never have let my mother… It won't happen again."

She finally looked at him, his strong chin and pointy nose. He put his hand on her cheek and my heart just about stopped. If I had any control over this situation we would've been making out with this Disney prince already. But Bessie was stubborn.

She pulled away. "The opinions of others will always matter to a weak person."

Ouch. I doubted there'd be a kiss now. *Way to blow it, Cinderella.*

His face dropped. "I came here to apologize."

"Not necessary," she spat. "What's done is done. I'm leaving for Europe next week."

His face fell, eyes widened. "I'll go too."

"Don't bother. I'm well aware of the real reason you came here tonight. You thought I'd be too stupid in love to realize it. But I'm not. This is just another sad attempt to get the business deal going again."

"It's not."

"Only because I'm not allowing it. I played the part of the stupid girl once. That part can go to someone else now."

He chugged the rest of his champagne and threw his glass into the parking lot area, watching it crash along a rock somewhere.

Shoving his hat on, he stormed out to the field of cars and

buggies, kicking pebbles and rocks along the way. He didn't look back.

As soon as he was out of sight, instead of walking inside, Bessie downed her champagne and set her glass on the rock by her feet. It was surreal seeing it there, knowing there was a photo of it hanging in the bed and breakfast. There would soon be a mysterious driving glove joining it later after her death. The distraught party guest.

Her eyes watered. Her chest heaved in short bursts.

"That must've been very hard to do," I said.

"Pretending you don't care always is," she replied. "It was better for the both of us, really, even if he was telling the truth. If we'd have married, he'd have spent every waking moment wondering what it was like to have children."

"I'm sorry," I said, mostly because it was all I could think to say. "You weren't too old to have children, though."

She went on. "Truth is, I didn't want them. I was afraid of them. Worried I'd be a horrible mother, like my own mother and sister. I resented my mother because she let the housekeeper raise us. My sister resented her own children because she didn't have a housekeeper to raise them and had to do all her own work."

She looked out at the darkened trees around us, illuminated only by the lantern decorations surrounding the front lawn. Nothing seemed very festive anymore.

Out of the corner of my eye, I thought I saw a dark figure dart through the trees beside us. It looked like an animal, or a man. It was too fast for me to see anything but a shadow. It was heading toward the back of the house.

"Did you see that?"

"See what?" she asked.

"Is your room back there?"

"Of course. Why?"

"I saw someone or something running back there. Let's go see if it was your killer," I said, even though I knew that investigating dark figures was an impossibility. I was reliving a memory, not creating one. And all Bessie could do at this moment was lean against the oak and gulp in as much of a deep breath as her corset would allow. She did not look over toward the woods again.

"Who knew about the window not latching right?" I asked Bessie, as we trudged inside, our heavy footfalls echoing off the planks of the porch.

"I'm not sure. Only family and Walter, I think," she replied.

As soon as the door creaked open, the music stopped. All eyes were on us, causing the announcer to clap his hands vigorously. "There's our guest of honor now. Who's ready for cake?"

Bessie was taken by surprise. She dabbed at her makeup and sniffed back her tears, searching the crowd for a familiar face, anyone to turn to, to lean on.

In less than a minute, three men in tuxedos wheeled a large three-tiered cake lit with candles across the dance floor. Thirty-five long candles sparkling in the dim room. Bessie's parents, and her sister joined her by the cake.

Before she could say anything, her father aimed her attention to a man behind a tripod where an unusually large black camera had been positioned. Bessilyn forced her mouth to smile.

As soon as the flash popped, I felt an odd connection to the photo along the back wall of the bed and breakfast where everyone else but Bessilyn had been smiling. Now, I knew the story behind her sadness.

Someone began singing "For she's a jolly good fellow..." and Bessie's face felt hot, flustered.

"I knew I was expected to make a speech," she said to me in her head as she stared at the burning candles. "All I wanted to do was run up to my room and hide."

But at the end of the song and the applause, she turned dutifully to the audience.

"Thank you all for coming," she said, making a wish and

blowing out the candles. "As you all know I'll be going on a very long trip soon, so this is also, I suppose, farewell for a while…"

"Proving that the Hinds will pay whatever it takes to get rid of their disgrace," a loud drunken voice rang out from the crowd. A few people in the crowd giggled awkwardly. Bessie turned toward the outburst. It was Troy. He staggered across the dance floor and over to the cake.

CHAPTER 8

FINAL MOMENTS

*B*essie swallowed. "Ladies and gentlemen, the man I'll miss the least when I go on my European trip, my sister's husband, Troy Brillows."

Troy teetered. His sunken face contorted in a smug sort of snarl. "At least Pleasant's married."

"Congratulations on being the least part of everyone's life."

Bessie's mother, a small, frail woman whose dress looked like it weighed more than she did, grabbed Bessie by the wrist and pulled her down to her height, whispering into her ear. "Go on up to your room now, Bessilyn, and wait for your father and me. We have a lot to discuss with you. The party's wrapping up, anyway."

Bessie gave her mother a look. But her mother's face, which had almost no color left, told her she should do as she was told.

"This is when they kill me," she said to me in her head. "I'm almost certain now. They blamed me for the deal falling through, even though they were the ones who ended it. I should've played my fiancee part better: contrite, well spoken, dainty."

She looked around at her party. "Thank you all again," she said out loud. "I'm feeling tired now. My mother just reminded me that I should really rest up for my long journey. Enjoy the cake." She tried to get herself to look around the room, to meet the eyes of the people who were not really her friends. No one looked back at her.

With a forced smile, she walked over to the stairs. Her drunken brother-in-law elbowed her on the way by him. A sharp pain went up her arm.

"Folks, let's hear it for my wife's pathetic, spinster sister," he said, applauding; a lit cigarette dangled from his fingers sending ash off in different directions.

Before I knew what was happening, Bessie ran at him, shoving him as hard as she could and, in his drunken state, that was all it took. He spun a 180 and smashed head first into the cake before landing onto the dance floor.

The crowd erupted into a mix of gasps and laughter. Bessie hurried up the stairs, barely able to hold in her smile as her parents yelled how she was too old for this.

We brushed by a woman in a short black dress. She turned toward us on the stairs and my thoughts went blank. It was me. Eliza, actually.

"Excuse me," she said, looking straight into Bessie's eyes for what seemed like a full minute. I studied the lines and contours of my own face, my hazel eyes, the soft wine color of my lips. It was strange being face to face with my identical twin, in a short black cocktail dress that seemed completely inappropriate for such a conservative era. She studied Bessie in the same way I was studying her, like she could see all the way through to Bessilyn's soul, maybe even to me, piggybacking on this memory. "It's you," she said, and I screamed a little in Bessie's head.

She sees me.

I couldn't look away. Eliza put her hand on Bessie's arm and Bessie's muscles tightened under the stranger's touch.

"You're the birthday girl," Eliza finally said in a voice just like my own. She pointed back toward the mess being cleaned up at the bottom of the stairs where Troy was still yelling about the spinster. "Nice birthday present to yourself." She winked. "Best party I've been to all year."

Bessie nodded her thanks. And Eliza went up the stairs, leaving us dumbfounded.

"Did that happen the first time?" I asked. "Or did we just create a new memory within a memory?"

"I don't know," Bessie admitted. "I don't think I would've remembered it if it had happened, not with everything else going on."

Bessie ran up the stairs just in time to catch a glimpse of Eliza heading into a room off the back of the hall.

"Where's she going?" I asked.

"That's the bathroom."

I knew that was the end of the memory I'd get with Eliza. It had been way too short, and really hadn't told me anything about the curse. I shook myself out of my disappointment. I had a job to do.

Bessie opened her bedroom door. "It's time," she said to me.

Her room was the largest bedroom I'd ever seen, luxurious yet cozy with a fireplace along one of the walls. But I didn't envy a 30-something living with her parents, no matter how wonderful the accommodations. I used to be that girl, living in my mother's basement.

Bessie flopped on her perfectly made white bedspread. "I know you're not a detective," she said. "But does anyone besides my parents seem suspicious to you?"

"Everyone does, Bessie," I replied. "Honestly. Your brother-in-law, of course. Your parents. Your parents' friends, the suffragist haters. But I have to admit. Sir Walter seems the most likely."

"W-what?"

"Think about it. You two got into an argument. He ran off. Then, a suspicious figure scurried off in the shadows toward the back of your house, over to your room, probably to climb a trellis he's very familiar with and a window he knows doesn't latch."

"That does make sense," she said. "I'm sure his family blamed him for the deal falling through. He was sent here to court me for that reason alone."

"I don't believe that. And neither do you." I scanned the room. "Let's review our other clues. You didn't lock the door just now. And I remember from the article in Henry Bowman's scrapbook that you were found shot in the heart with the door locked, which was why it was ruled a suicide."

I thought I heard something outside her door, so I listened more intensely, looking around at the details in the room. A pamphlet about the suffrage movement sat on her nightstand. Her armoire was open, and on the top shelf, a gun. *The gun.* The one in Paula Henkel's display case.

It was strange waiting for the final moment, recounting the details like they were some sort of sick check list.

Bessie unlaced her black boots and plopped into bed, pulling the covers over her face so I couldn't see anything anymore. Her nose was stuffing up. Tears were streaming down her eyes, along her cheeks.

There was a light knock at the door.

"You okay, missy?" a woman's voice on the other side said. The door creaked open. "You want some warm milk? And your special pills for sleeping?"

Bessie peeked out over the covers. An older woman with pale puffy eyes and saggy cheeks poked her head inside the room, dressed in a long black dress and white apron, the Hind family housekeeper, probably.

"Oh honey," she said when she saw Bessie crying. The woman set the glass of milk down and rushed to the bed, stroking Bessie's hair, pulling it free from its proper up-do and running her fingers through it. "You know I always cry on my birthday too, I do. Every year like clockwork. Mostly because it starts to become depressing the older you get when you ain't got nothing but age to show for it. But you? You're still young and rich. You're a lucky woman."

"Thanks, Martha," Bessie said, sitting up. Martha handed Bessilyn the milk and dropped two little pills into her hand. Bessie gulped them down, wiping her mouth with a handkerchief on the side of the table. "Sir Walter was there," she said to her housekeeper.

"He was? I didn't notice. Stand up and I'll help you out of that corset."

"Not yet," Bessilyn said, lying back down. "I'm not sure I'm ready to end my night."

"But you took your pills."

"I know. I'm feeling a little confused."

"Men'll do that to you," Martha said, sitting down next to us. "Tell me. Did he look good?"

Bessie smiled. "Too good. He wanted to get back together. He said he loved me."

"Then why are you up here crying?"

Bessie played with the sleeves of her stiff dress. "I'm not sure I believed him."

"Poor, silly girl. A man sneaks into a party when he knows he's not wanted. That's love."

"Is that what love is? I always wondered."

Martha stood up and looked around the room, shaking her head at he mess as she snatched clothes from off the floor left and right, balling them along her arm.

"I guess you know what happened downstairs," Bessie said, watching as her housekeeper tidied up after her. "Sorry for making such a mess with the cake. I'm too old for that."

"I was upstairs when it happened, but don't worry, miss. It's not your fault."

"Yes, it was. I shoved Troy into the cake."

Martha let out a loud, long cackle. "You don't say? Now,

there's a mess I don't mind cleaning up."

"My parents are going to kill me. We're about to be the talk of the town."

"Don't you know? That's why people have parties in the first place. They want to be the talk of the town. A party is only as good as the gossip that comes out of it." She turned her head from side to side and lowered her voice. "And I have my own bit of gossip from the party," she said.

Bessie leaned her head against her headboard as the woman continued.

"Just now, I walked in on Mr. Henry Bowman and the woman he always goes 'round with. The one who is not his wife. They was in the bathroom together."

"You don't say. What happened?" Bessie yawned and closed her eyes.

The woman's voice went sheepish. "I'll tell you later, missy." She kissed the top of Bessie's head. "You sure you don't want me to help you get out of your party clothes?"

"Not yet. I'm starving, Martha. I didn't eat a bite all night."

"I told you that corset was too tight."

"Stop lecturing me, and be a dear. See if you can bring me a plate. And let me know if Sir Walter's still around."

"Now I see why you're keeping your clothes on." Martha was at the dresser now, pouring water onto what appeared to be a cloth. She handed it to Bessie, and like a nightly ritual, she immediately put it over her eyes. The cool cloth felt good.

"You rest your eyes. I'll... I'll... what in the world..." Martha's voice trailed off in different pitches, like she was moving around the room.

"What is it?" Bessie asked. She pulled the cloth off and sat up.

"Nothing," Martha said, smiling. "I'll see what I can bring you. I only hope I can do it without Esther seeing me. Your sister has her watching those devil kids of hers, and I know that poor girl's looking for me to relieve her."

That got Bessie laughing a little as the housekeeper closed the door and hustled away.

Bessie's head throbbed with a headache. She flicked off the light and pulled the cool wet cloth back over her eyes.

I wanted to hear the gossip about Henry Bowman and Eliza, but I knew it was impossible. The end was coming soon, and I had to keep my focus. Our eyes were shut and she was starting to fade into the forced sleep from her pills, so I tried to use my other senses: smell, hearing, touch...

I didn't hear much. Maybe the door, ever so light, not like the heavy creak when the housekeeper entered... maybe the window, maybe the door locking, liquid sloshing...

Something scratchy suddenly clamped over Bessie's mouth. We squirmed into the fumes that surrounded us, strong and sweet. Bessie pulled her head to one side then the other, trying to cough or gasp, trying to move away, but the force had her pinned. She grabbed at the hand over her mouth, leathery and thick. Her mind was succumbing to the total darkness that consumed us. Her resistance lessened. And then, nothing. I knew she'd blacked out. But I also knew from my other experience with channeling that I didn't need to. I wouldn't be able to see, but I could still narrow in on my other senses.

The pressure released from Bessie's mouth, and I focused on her breath, slow yet shallow. Sounds were all around me. A door locking. Heavy breathing. Footsteps, first slow then faster. Pacing maybe. Whoever it was sounded like they were having second thoughts. I tried to concentrate on one of the sounds. It was like cloth, moving... odd.

A gush of wind blew over my face and an owl hooted off in the distance. The window was opening; I could tell.

I heard several clicks before something pressed hard against my heart. I didn't have time to brace myself, a loud explosive pop followed.

And I woke in my living room. The images of the channeling already falling into a distant, blurry memory.

Snapping myself out of it, I quickly ran to the kitchen and threw open the pantry. Stale Pringles and a Diet Coke were perfect right now. Not exactly gourmet-whatever in burgundy sauce, but it would do. I grabbed my phone and my channeling notebook from the dining room then curled up on the settee. It was 12:30. I'd been channeling for more than three hours. I was starving. My body ached, and my eyelids felt like they outweighed me, but I had to get the experience down before I forgot it all.

I stuffed a full-inch stack of Pringles in my mouth. Crumbs spilled onto my phone as I looked up clues while scribbling things into my notebook. Bessilyn had already been pretty drugged up with her sleeping pills when whoever the killer was pressed a towel over her face. And from my cursory internet search, I decided that towel must have been full of chloroform. The only other clues I remembered from the moments right before death were the rustling of what sounded like cloth and a window opening. I wondered if the latch on the window also locked from the outside.

It must have. Did the shadowy figure I saw on the side of the house sneak up the trellis and wait in Bessie's room for her that night? And who would have access to chloroform, anyway? Even in 1906, that must've been hard to come by.

Jackson appeared as I guzzled down my soda.

"You okay?" he said in such a way that made me question it myself.

I nodded. "I know she's resting from the channeling, but as soon as you see Bessilyn, let her know I have a million questions for her."

"You should rest too," Jackson said. I rolled my eyes and chugged down some more soda.

CHAPTER 9

THE UNUSUAL SUSPECTS

*B*oth of Potter Grove's police cars were parked at awkward angles along the entrance to the Purple Pony when I got there the next day for work. My heart raced. Whatever was going on had to be serious.

My mind was numb, but I knew it wasn't just because I was worried. It had been surreal, dying in 1906 just last night only to be jolted awake in the present. After scribbling everything down into my notebook, I hadn't gotten much sleep. And now I felt older, stiffer, and more than a little off.

My pace picked up the closer I got to the entrance. I could see the quaint little hippie shop had been ransacked. Justin stood leaning against the entrance as I approached, glitter from the aging unicorn over his head was all in his hair like sparkly purple dandruff.

"Is she okay?" I asked, searching his eyes to see if he was worried.

"Yes," he replied. "She's fine. Her shop's not, though. Somebody's trashed it." He looked at me like he wanted to say something else. I knew it was just the usual, weird heaviness that floated between us from the past we pretended not to have together.

I walked past him and went inside. I wasn't sure how I felt about him yet, but I was sure glad I was wearing my cute skinny jeans that made my butt look good.

As soon as I stepped inside, I could see Justin had not been exaggerating about the place being trashed. Even some of Rosalie's paintings were ripped to shreds, pieces of them hanging off the toppled racks like cobwebs. The jewelry section was a mess. Gems and polished stones were strewn all over the floor. I almost slipped on them on my way over to Rosalie, who was sitting on one of her stools, her dreadlocks completely disheveled. Some dreadlocks were in a ponytail, some out. She clutched at her heart. Caleb had his notebook out. I knew he was probably why her heart was acting up.

"What in the world happened?" I asked.

"She's a little shook up," he replied to me. "She *claims* a wild animal was here when she came out of the back room, but she can't describe the animal. Supposedly, the place looked just like this."

"Supposedly?" I said.

"She wouldn't be the first person with a failing business to commit insurance fraud," he replied.

I threw my hands on my hips. "Just jot down your information and keep your opinions to yourself, officer."

Justin scooted by the sheriff to get closer to Rosalie. When he passed, I noticed he also had purple unicorn glitter all along the backside of his uniform too. The outside doorframe was not a safe place to lean against around here. I stopped myself from brushing it off of him.

"You sure you don't want me to take you to the hospital," he asked my boss.

She shook her head *no.* I knew Rosalie would rather bleed to death than go to one of those places.

"Do you think this is the same animal that scared Delilah Scott?" I asked.

Justin shrugged. "Sure looks like an animal did this."

"All I know is... Rosalie said, her voice quick and raspy. "I heard growling somewhere around the window. I couldn't tell if it was inside or out, so I ran into the back room. What else could I do? And that's where I stayed for a full hour until Paula Henkel came in."

She motioned to the chair by the dressing room, and I looked over, finally noticing the dreadful woman sitting there, scrolling on her phone. She smiled and smugly waved to me, her teeth perfectly white and straight, her smile calm.

She waltzed over. "Good thing I came over right on time," she said, stuffing her phone in her bra. She put her hand on Rosalie's shoulder, and Rosalie flinched. "I'm just glad I could help, that's all." Her tone had that dramatic sweetness to it that people used when they weren't really being sweet.

"Why are you here anyway," I asked.

"Rosalie told me to come at 11:00. She wanted to cancel the seance and I told her we should talk about it this morning. But when I got here, I saw the store in shambles. So I found Rosalie and called the police. You're welcome, by the way."

"Yes, thank you for all your *help*," I said. "But, if you're done helping, I got it from here. You can take off."

She curled her thin lip up. "Sheriff, am I free to leave?"

"You can go," he said, closing up his notebook. "I think we have enough information."

Paula turned back around before she left. "Funny. I was just texting another medium before you came in. She's willing to take over the seance if you both are serious about canceling."

"Now's not a good time," I said. "But yeah, we cancelled. The other medium can have it. Did you tell her you're selling tickets all over town, making a bundle while paying the mediums nothing?"

"I wouldn't call hundreds of dollars nothing. Would you?" Paula turned to the police. They didn't say anything.

She looked about half the size of the deputy she was standing by as she paused at the front door. "I just want to point out that I came over here an hour after this store opened. One hour. I was your first customer, not that I was actually buying anything."

She pushed her lips together, tried to look concerned. "I know this is a bad time, and I don't want to tell you how to run your business, but it seems like you could use the publicity that this seance would bring you. A lot of people are interested. And you'll probably get quite a bit on the backend selling, oh I don't know, whatever you people sell — gems or incense or something. Maybe you should think long term and not just immediate gains for once."

I waved. "Good bye. We're fine. Thanks for your concern."

"Give me your answer by six o'clock this evening or I'm going with the other medium."

"We've already given you our answer. More than once now. We cancelled. End of story," I yelled as she left. I turned to my boss and put my hand on her shoulder. She didn't cringe this time. "Why don't you go on home. I'll clean up here and take over the shop."

She hugged me tightly, grabbing my arm and using it to help her hobble off the stool. She limped to the back room and I followed. As soon as we were alone in the back, I whispered. "Are you really okay?"

"Yes, except Paula Henkel and Caleb Bowman were here for far too long." She held her chest again. "You know I'm too old for that. My damn heart can't take but five minutes of certain damn people."

She was cussing again, and I was pretty sure five more minutes with those two and she would've been dropping f-bombs.

She gathered up some scattered papers that were laying

around the back table and put them in her purse. One of them was a ticket to the seance.

"Fancy, huh?" she said, handing me the gold and silver embossed 4x5 ticket. It had been printed on heavy card stock. "Paula gave it to me. Just now, while we were talking to the police. Can you believe it?"

"Tacky," I said.

"She said we could get in to the dinner for free if we worked the seance. Like that shouldn't have been part of the deal in the first place."

I handed the ticket back to Rosalie. "I'm glad you cancelled. Look how large our names are. She wants us. We're a draw here in Potter Grove. The women from the country club who come in here... they love you."

Rosalie looked down at the card in her hand. "Nobody comes in much anymore. And truth is, I could use the business."

I didn't tell her this, but I needed it too, for my case. The bed and breakfast was where Bessie died and where she haunted. And I was pretty sure there was a reason Sir Walter felt familiar to me in the channeling. I was almost certain his presence had been the male presence I'd felt at the bed and breakfast.

"I'll go see her when I get off work," I said. "I'll tell her we want half the ticket sales. She can keep the dinner profit."

"She's not gonna agree to that."

"The hell she won't. She'll have to reprint everything if she goes with the new medium."

Caleb poked his head into the back room. His voice was slow and drawn out. "Rosalie, I'm leavin'. Keep your doors closed from now on, okay? Wild animals can get in when the door's left open," he said in a slow tone, like we were all as dumb as wild animals over here.

"The door was closed," Rosalie said.

He threw her a condescending smirk. "According to Paula

Henkel, when she got here, the front door was propped open, remember?" He shook his head and left.

Rosalie lowered her voice as soon as he was gone. "I can't prove anything, but I think Paula's behind this."

"Maybe," I said. "But it also could've been a wild animal."

Rosalie's normally pale face grew red. "By the time Paula called me back last night, I'd already asked all over town. I knew she was making bank on this thing, so I told her we needed fifty percent of everything or the deal was off. Especially for an audience that large."

"How large?" I asked, my heart pounding.

"She wouldn't say, but at the rate they're selling, probably expect about a hundred. I tried to call you last night."

I sat down at her desk. I couldn't tell Rosalie the reason I hadn't picked up was because I was busy doing a channeling with Bessilyn Hind. She was already pretty shook up, and I didn't want her worrying about me at a time like this. She thought channeling was dangerous, and I was fine. Probably.

Rosalie was still talking. "So we got into it on the damn phone last night. We were supposed to work out all the damn terms this morning."

"And then this happened," I said. "That's some interesting damn timing."

Rosalie nodded.

CHAPTER 10

ON DISPLAY

*L*ater that afternoon, Shelby stumbled into the Purple Pony, practically dragging a newborn baby carrier. I was just finishing inventorying all the damaged merchandise from the pile I'd created on the checkout counter when I noticed her. I rushed to hold the door open.

Every few steps, she'd stop and put the carrier down, take a deep breath then pick it back up again. When she turned the car seat around, I saw why she was struggling. Every inch of that carrier had been taken up by the largest baby head I'd ever seen, peeking out from a gray blanket. Thick cheeks and a round ruddy expression that looked like it might gobble up anything that got too close to its mouth.

I'd just seen Bobby Jr. a week ago, and he looked like he'd doubled in size since then, or at least his head had. Largest one-month-old head ever.

"I swear, every day he looks more and more like his daddy. Don't you think," Shelby said.

"Come on, now," I said. "This baby's cute." She gave me a look so I had to say I was joking.

She told me all about how she and Bobby were about to celebrate their one-year proposal anniversary, and Bobby was planning something special.

"Like a wedding?"

"Don't rush us," she said. "We're getting to that. But I am honestly in no hurry to have a third husband. I don't know where he's taking me, though. It's a surprise..." she stopped mid-sentence and looked around at the mess on the floor and the counter. "What happened here?" she asked.

The humungous baby head was smiling at me, and I barely looked up from it when I told Shelby about Delilah Scott hearing a growling noise and what had happened with Rosalie. Like a punch in my empty uterus, my baby instincts were kicking in.

"So, they think a wild animal is running around town?"

I shrugged. "Probably just shapeshifters."

"That's not funny. Everyone knows that's only a rumor, thank goodness." She shivered. "Whatever it is, it sounds like it's in this neighborhood. Aren't you the least bit afraid?"

I thought about that a second. I should have been, I guess. It wasn't like I was raised on weapons. My mother had been an engineer in Indianapolis. She tried to teach me things like rewiring circuit boards, (which after the fifth time, I would just nod and say I had it). And, I didn't have a dad. "I guess there's nothing to do except keep the doors shut and my eyes open," I said.

"I'm gonna get some bear spray. That's what I'm gonna do. You should get some too," she said, dragging the baby carrier back toward the door again, looking around as she did. "I never told anyone this, but I've had this feeling for a while. Something in Potter Grove isn't safe."

"Yeah," I said. "I'm pretty sure that's the town's new motto."

AFTER WORK, I found myself sitting in my car at the bed and

breakfast, rehearsing all the different ways I might be able to negotiate with an awful woman. I glanced out my window, catching something large and furry in the shadows around the side of the house. It moseyed around the back before I could get too much of a look at it, though, making me wonder if I'd really even seen anything.

I opened the car door and practically fell out of it.

Maybe that was the wild animal that had trashed the Purple Pony.

The sun was just setting and the shadows of dusk could've been playing tricks on my mind, or so I told myself. A cool September breeze blew through my curls, and I pulled my jacket in tighter as I followed the animal, pushing my camera app on, already counting the money I was going to get from the first good picture of Big Foot.

I followed the decorative stone around toward the back, looking in all directions, listening as I walked. Shelby's words echoed through my head, "Something in Potter Grove isn't safe."

The sound of that something sloshing through wet earth made me momentarily gasp until I realized it was my new boots slipping through the bed and breakfast's manicured lawn. Apparently, for my $10, I'd also received a weird suction-cup sound included with my no-traction boots.

I stopped just before I reached the back of the house and listened for a second. *A low guttural growl.*

My heart felt like it was going to pound its way out of my jacket and I tried to get my hands to stop shaking so I could get a good picture. No wonder all the photos were blurry.

I backed away just as a shadow came closer. Screaming louder than I'd intended, I dropped my phone and ran. Something else screamed back.

I turned back around to see what it was. Paula Henkel.

"What is wrong with you?" she said, coming out from the back, her arms full of firewood.

"You didn't see or hear anything? Like a wild animal? I thought I heard growling."

"Sure you did. You and your boss."

I looked all around the back yard. There was nothing back there, except a manmade pond and a gazebo. I flashed back to the night before. This was the part of the yard where Sir Walter and Bessilyn had had their argument. To my right was where the rock used to be, the one where Bessie set her champagne glass down.

"Don't tell me. You've come to say you want your job back," she said, smugly carrying her firewood over to the entrance. I wasn't sure how she managed to do everything smugly, but she did.

I didn't answer as I followed her inside. Every part of me hated the fact I had to ask for this.

Inside was warm, the fire toasty. She put the logs on the hearth as I looked around. The bed and breakfast seemed different to me than it had in the channeling last night. The then-and-now differences were huge, even though Paula had made an attempt to recreate them. The furniture set-up was all different, and the chandelier was gone. It probably should've felt cheerier with the new colors and the bright lighting, but it just felt pit-of-my-stomach hollow and sad. Maybe channeling was harder on my psyche than I thought it'd be. Maybe I was just missing that corset.

There was a new display now. Another glass museum-like enclosure at the front of the room by the check-in counter, where a black felt bowler hat sat on a stand, a description typed on card stock underneath it. It read:

Love Can Make You Lose Your Hat...
This bowler hat was a popular style in 1906 when it was found outside
Hind House on the night rich socialite and philanthropist Bessilyn
Margaret Hind took her own life at her birthday party. The hat
belonged to millionaire Sir Walter Timbre, Bessilyn's fiancee, who told

police he lost it during a heated argument with Bessilyn when she begged him to come back and they broke up for good. With her prospects for marriage ending, the despondent 35-year-old suffragist and women's rights leader retired to her room where she shot herself in the heart.

"Like my display? I just got it."

I nodded, even though I was pretty sure Bessie was going to lose her hat when she saw it.

Paula motioned around at the decor of the lobby. "It really adds to the ambiance of the business, huh?" She leaned in and lowered her voice like we were sharing a secret. "I'm not just selling a cozy place to spend the night anymore. That was the old bed and breakfast and that's why they went out of business. I'm selling death, and the stories that go with it."

"Where did you get all your display stuff?" I asked.

She smiled, obviously thinking I was impressed with her morbid marketing skills, which I absolutely was.

"The police," she said. "If you can believe it. All by accident. I was talking to the sheriff about how I thought the bed and breakfast might be haunted by Bessie Hind, and he told me they still had some of her stuff in their old evidence locker. He wasn't even sure why they had it there. It was a routine case. Sometimes, I feel like the luckiest person alive."

She went on, telling me all about how she purchased the items for a steal from the police department, and the huge amount she estimated their real worth to be. "Of course, I had to make Caleb think he was raking me over the coals…"

"So, did Sir Walter really say this to the police?"

She looked at me sideways, probably because I was more interested in what a dead man said to the police 100-something years ago than how much money she was going to make off the dead man's hat.

"It was in the police report. Why?"

"Do you have that report? I didn't see it in the display."

"I was thinking about adding it, but not until it gets some work done. It's faded and disintegrating."

I just decided to tell her the truth. "I don't think Bessilyn Hind killed herself. I'm going to try to prove it, and solve her murder."

She rolled her eyes like I was joking.

I went on. "The mere fact the police department had this stuff in evidence, that they took pictures and documented witnesses, says someone there thought something seemed off about her suicide."

"I don't think it matters too much anymore."

"Maybe only to the people selling tickets." I winked. "It's an interesting angle. You have to admit."

Her jaw moved back and forth under her smile.

I tried to feel the room for that same familiar presence as before, but I couldn't really pick up on anything, just a quiet stirring. "I think Sir Walter Timbre is here too," I said. "It might be fun to ask him about the police report. Don't you think? Maybe solve Bessie's murder at the seance."

I thought I heard a cash register ca-ching-ing away in the woman's head. "You want me to go get the police report? It's just upstairs in my room."

That stocky woman could sure move fast when marketing was on the line. She hustled up the stairs, rubbing her hands together. Apparently, we both needed this seance to be a hit.

Attached to the pedestal, beside the bowler hat, was a slightly enlarged photo of Sir Walter. It was the exact one from the microfilm. And I tried, once again, to make contact with the gorgeous man.

Orchestra music played softly from a stereo somewhere nearby, a nice touch but a little out of era from the music I remembered that night. "Sir Walter," I whispered into the living room. I went over to Bessie's display, just to see the glove again. I forced myself to look at the dress too. The lace that had trimmed the bodice area hung free on one side and a large brown stain covered the heart area. I looked away. Even though it was more than 100 years ago and everyone who was at Bessie's party was now deceased, the finality of that one moment — the second between life and death, now finely pressed and on display — made me understand the disdain most of the dead seemed to have for the living, even though they'd all been living once too. We did seem to have problems keeping our priorities straight.

Paula fast walked back into the room, a Ziploc bag dangling from her hand. She held it out for me, but when I went to take it, she pulled it back. "Sorry," she said. "This is a great angle, and I truly believe this might bring in a larger draw, but you and Rosalie cancelled on me. This isn't *your* seance. Thank you for the idea, though. I will tell the new medium to see what she thinks."

"I've done a ton of research on this thing. I… I…" I stopped short of telling her I had Bessilyn Hind staying at my house and that I'd already done a channeling with her.

"You… you what? You bring in a big crowd? Bessilyn Hind is what people are coming to see. Any monkey can perform the show. You're welcome to buy a ticket, though," she said. "Tell Rosalie the one I gave her isn't valid anymore."

A young couple came through the front door, carrying shopping bags and saying, "hello" at pretty much the same time.

The woman had the longest straightest jet-black hair I'd ever seen. It was pretty much the opposite of her partner's bright orange spiky do.

The woman stared at me. "You're Carly Taylor, aren't you?"

I smirked at Paula Henkel. "Why yes, I am." I wondered if the new medium was going to be as easily recognizable to strangers.

"I'm Emerald and this is my husband, Dragon Fire." She pulled an EMF reader from one of her bags and started waving it around the room. "I looked you up as soon as we were asked to take over the seance from you."

I could hardly believe Emerald and Dragon Fire were about to see Sir Walter's evidence, and I wasn't.

The woman put the reader over by Walter's display. "Yes, I'm picking up very specific energy here, Ms. Hind. I will definitely be able to sign an agreement that says Bethany Henkel will be here for the seance coming up."

I headed for the door but hesitated at the knob. "You guys didn't hear a large animal growling out here, did you?"

Dragon Fire looked at me like I was crazy. "No."

"You will if you cancel."

Paula shouted to me as I left. "Tell Rosalie I want my book back. Landover County: Then and Now. I only gave it to her so you'd know who Bessilyn Hind was."

"Don't you mean Bethany Henkel? You all have a wonderful seance."

CHAPTER 11

CROOKED

I had the next day off, which was unfortunate because it was a Thursday, one of the days my creepy house-keeper checked on the house.

I tried to look the part of comfortable, sitting on the couch, while Mrs. Harpton moved at break-neck speed around me, like a black tornado of motion. She swirled around from room to room, making checks on how I was keeping the place while she dusted here and swept there.

It was all part of the stack of paperwork I had to sign as part of my inheritance. From what time I put the dishes away to the temperature of Rex's dog's food, I had to do everything perfectly.

And I was pretty far from perfect. I caught quite a few scowls from my housekeeper, but then, it might just have been the dress she was wearing. I'd scowl too if I had to wear something that went all the way up my neck and seemed to be made from what-ever that awful material is that umbrellas are made out of.

Somehow, I got it in my head that I wanted to touch it.

I'd long suspected the woman was a ghost. I never saw her coming or going. And she looked like she'd stepped out of a 19th century funeral home. But she was the most human-looking ghost I'd ever seen, if she was one. I needed to know. Plus, other people (people who did not have a strong mediumship like I did) could see her too.

When she was busy in the living room fluffing up the pillows on the settee, I pretended to be interested in the vase on the coffee table. But as soon as I got about an inch from her skirt, she practically flew away with such accuracy and dexterity I felt like I was moving in slow motion compared to her. I tried again in the dining room to touch her skirt and got a little closer that time. But once again, I was no match. It was like chasing a hummingbird.

"You slow me down," she finally said. "I can be done in five minutes. Go."

It was a silly game anyway. I threw open the cabinet in the pantry and yanked two keys from their hooks. "I'll be in the library if you need me," I said to the blur. I knew it was the one place Mrs. Harpton wouldn't touch. Plus, I'd been so caught up in Bessie and solving her murder, I hadn't had time to look through my new scrapbook yet.

I whistled for Rex on my way out to the veranda. But just like my ex, he usually hid when Mrs. Harpton was cleaning. He hated going to the turret, anyway, even before the incident with Brock. I couldn't blame him. The main turret was one of the strangest parts of this house. Just off the veranda, it had its own entrance and lock. And, it had been designed on purpose to look like two turrets from the outside, one on top of the other, lopsided. It was just a small part of the oddities of Gate House, though.

My favorite oddity was the one just across from the creepy nursery on the second floor, a door that led to no place. Just a wall. There was another one of those down the hall near the basement too. The house also featured fireplaces with no chimneys. And chimneys with no fireplaces. And a weird dead horse art piece with its tongue hanging out in the nursery because what says "Good night, sleep tight, kiddo" more than that?

My ex-husband was waiting for me, legs crossed on the red sofa, when I got up to the third floor of the turret. "What took you so long? This is where I live on Mondays and Thursdays," he said, laughing a little at the "lived" part. He was starting to gain more color, not nearly the amount that Bessie had, or Mrs. Harpton.

I nodded without saying anything else. I reached behind him, accidentally going through part of his shoulder, causing a cool breeze to shoot along my hand, as I grabbed my two scrapbooks from off the shelf. I set them on the coffee table in front of us.

Jackson turned to me. "Do you think you need the seance to figure out Bessie's murder? I heard you cancelled."

I shrugged. "I really wanted the money, though. But now, I want Bessie to stay as far away from that seance as possible. I've been replaced. And I want the seance to bomb."

"Oh goody. More time with the suffragist."

"I like her," I said, raising an eyebrow at my ex.

"I'm just tired of hearing about it, that's all. Did you know she was in charge of the women's rights movement here in Potter Grove? I only know because she mentions it every other second like she's expecting applause."

"So you're saying this house can only fit one large head at a time?"

"Precisely." He cupped his own chin. "And this adorable head was here first."

I thumbed through the new scrapbook as I talked, stopping on one of the 8x10 sepia photos of a large crow with thick, black, greasy-looking feathers.

"Your great grandfather was a loon. You know that, right," I said. "What is up with all these pictures of birds?"

He didn't answer. I didn't really expect him to.

The scrapbook seemed oddly familiar. I could almost guess

with astounding accuracy what the next photo was going to be every time I turned the page. But then, that's not as impressive as it sounds when "another black bird" was a solid guess. But it became a bit of a game, only ending when I said, "The back of a woman's head while she reads through her notes," while turning the page. I gasped when I saw I'd been right. Down to the little glass figurine sitting on the stack of papers by her typewriter.

How could I have known that? I shook it off and moved on. I must've already looked through this book and hadn't remembered. One of the pages caught my eye.

It was another photo of what looked like a classroom, the girls in curls and white dresses, the boys in black uniforms, hair perfectly combed to the side. I'd seen a similar photo in the other scrapbook.

I threw the first scrapbook open, the one I found the night I solved the stripper murders, and scanned its pages until I found the picture of the classroom.

The photos had to have been taken on the exact same day because the two adults standing off in the back of the room were the same. A man with a handlebar mustache that I now heavily suspected was Jackson's lawyer, Ronald, and a woman who looked a lot like Mrs. Harpton. The photos weren't exactly the same, though. The one in the new scrapbook was taken from a different angle.

And from that new side angle, I could see that the door in the back of the schoolroom was open. And, a horse sculpture hung on the wall of whatever room was across the hall from it. I studied it a second, my mouth falling open when I realized what it was.

Creepy bugged-out eyes and a tongue flopping out of an opened mouth. It had to be the same horse from the nursery upstairs. I squinted again. It had to be.

Could the schoolroom in this photo be located directly across from my own creepy nursery?

A chill went up my spine, making me aware of every hair on my neck when I thought about what was currently located across the hall from that nursery. The crazy door that opened to nothing. It didn't seem so crazy anymore. I wasn't sure how I was going to break into whatever secret room was hiding there without tearing open the drywall, but I was going to figure it out. This was proof that there used to be a room there. Maybe.

I closed the book so quickly I almost caught my finger in its heavy binding, realizing it also had an ominous title in beautifully scripted cursive scrawled across the cover, just like the other scrapbook… because it's perfectly normal to title your scrapbooks in Old English script. "Upon a Crooked Stile."

Jackson had disappeared long ago when I was thumbing through the bird photos, but I was pretty sure he was still here. "A stile's like a passageway, right?" I yelled into the air to my former English professor who was now my dead ex-husband.

He appeared in front of me, throwing me a dimpled smile. "Well, actually," he began, his voice thick with arrogance. "It's usually a specific passageway, like steps or a ladder that would allow humans to pass through to an area while not allowing animals to pass. I believe the word itself is German in origin, but I could be wrong…"

I knew I should've just looked it up. He enjoyed spewing knowledge way too much, the know-it-all.

He sat back down next to me, and I almost expected to feel the warmth of his body once again. The smell of his sweat. I took a deep inhale, but smelled nothing. I was getting used to nothing.

Was the door that led to the wall the crooked stile? A room boarded up so humans couldn't pass, but other entities could? I felt an electric spark traveling up my body. *Was I figuring out clues?*

The only other items in the scrapbook were equally as confusing, a few obituaries clipped from newspapers and some bird photos. The man sure liked his birds and his obits.

I thought about it. Maybe Henry Bowman suspected Bessie's passageway to death had been crooked too.

I shook my head. I was probably reading way too much into a dead guy's scrapbook. But, I was one-hundred percent sure there was a boarded up room on the other side of the nursery now. And I was going to break into it, as soon as my housekeeper left.

CHAPTER 12

A MESSY SITUATION

*R*ex took off down the hall as soon as he saw me peeling away at the paint and wallpaper.

"Go big or go home, huh?" I yelled to him as I peeled another chunk from the wall in the hall across from the nursery. It lifted like a dry, brittle fingernail. There was no turning back now.

Each layer of wallpaper seemed to reveal another layer, a different pattern, like a rotten onion.

Sweat dripped from my forehead even though it was ten degrees cooler in this hall than in any other place in the house. I closed the door to the nursery as I worked so I wouldn't accidentally see the weird horse or the doll that looked just like me. Or maybe, it was so they wouldn't see me.

The outer layer of paper in the hallway had been painted plain white. At first, I hadn't even noticed it was wallpaper. My original plan was to bust through the wall one whack at a time, yelling "Here's Johnny" as I went. But, just as I was about to swing away at the wall with the only thing I could find to do it (one of Jackson's old golf clubs), I noticed a crack in the paint up in the corner of the door frame that looked like a folded piece of paper screaming for me to pull on it.

I obliged, realizing immediately, it wasn't drywall, but wallpaper covered by white paint. It peeled away easily and almost completely, revealing an odd kind of scene underneath. Black bears in a weird dark pattern where some bears were upside down and twisted this way and that, falling through a forest of patterned trees. They weren't cute bears. These bears' mouths hung open and their backs appeared flattened, more like hollow skins used for rugs.

Something told me not to hack away in a hurry but to take each layer like a surgeon would, carefully removing it. Underneath the bears was a golden colored wallpaper with nests and baby birds. Mother birds flew toward the nests at varying angles. They appeared to be feeding their babies very large bones.

Another layer was gargoyle-looking griffin beasts sitting next to dolls with curly brownish-blonde hair. The doll from the nursery?

I knocked on the wall. It seemed hollow. And when I pulled back the wallpaper and saw white drywall underneath, I knew it was time.

I paused, holding the golf club high above my head.

I'd lived in this house for seven years when I was married to Jackson and it never occurred to me to tear this wall open. Any wall, for that matter. But something was compelling me to do it now, and with certainty, as if I knew it was meant to happen. Just as I was certain there would be a photo of a woman drinking tea while reading notes. How could I have known that? Who was I?

With as much force as I could muster, I swung away at the wall, one blow after another, right at the doll's head that looked oddly similar to my own. Drywall crumbled into my hair, falling along my face. The sound of thwacks echoing off the other walls filled my ears as dust covered my vision. I coughed, and wiped my nose, but I didn't stop. I couldn't stop. This was just the beginning.

After a few minutes of whacking away, my arms felt like they wanted to bolt from my body, and my eyes were filled with so much dust, I probably could've planted seeds in them.

I hadn't thought to use safety equipment like goggles or gloves. I tried not to think about the fact that this was a hundred-year-old house, and my lungs were probably filled with lead or asbestos or something equally as deadly.

I squinted through my dusty vision, smiling when I saw a hole was finally forming along the bottom of the wall. At least I had something to show for the mesothelioma I was probably giving myself.

I kicked my new boots along the crumbling plaster, surprised when I saw my foot go straight through with a crash that shook the floor a little. I pulled it out and kicked the wall again. This time it stuck, and I almost lost my balance trying to yank it free.

"Carly doll," a calm voice beside me said as I hopped around like a wounded animal. "You've been very busy this afternoon."

I coughed on the dust falling from my hair and looked over. I could barely see my ex hovering in the hall, watching me tug a foot awkwardly out of drywall. My black jeans were covered in plaster and wallpaper bits. "There's a room back there, Jackson."

"Well, it certainly looks like you're creating one," he said.

I picked up my phone and shined it into the hole I'd made with my foot. "It's too dark. I can't see anything."

"What are you hoping to find?"

"Answers," I said, grabbing a hold of a piece of the wall and yanking another chunk off. And another. Jackson didn't say anything. The only sounds came from me and the crunching of the wall breaking into bits. "I want answers. I know there's something in here I'm supposed to find. Probably. And after I'm done here, I'm going to Indianapolis. I'm no longer waiting for my mother to tell me what she knows about my adoption. I'm going there and I'm going to demand she tell me."

"Sounds like a fool-proof plan. She won't be able to say 'no,' poor thing."

I hated it when he was right. It was a stupid idea.

The plaster came off pretty easily now. I gave it another kick, my foot crunching out more of a hole. I wiped my brow with the back of my hand, blinking away the dust falling along my lashes. "She probably thought she was helping me by sparing me the details of my adoption, by giving me the right education and nagging me to make traditional choices in life like career, marriage, and kids. It was a good plan..." I tossed another chunk of wall onto the huge pile forming in the hallway. My breath was heavy as I tried to talk and do hard labor at the same time. "But nothing ever works like you plan it to in life."

"Unless your plan is to make a mess."

I looked around at the mess beside me. Chunks of drywall, paint, and wallpaper cluttered the entire hallway from the maid's quarter's to the nursery.

My back muscles spasmed and my head throbbed. I sat down by the pile and rested my head against the good part of the wall.

Jackson sat down beside me, brushing my hair from my eyes, which felt a lot like a fan blowing it. "You know what's funny," he said, turning his head to the side so I would catch his eye. "It's only after you die that you realize there are no real answers in life."

"Oh good. The meaning of life is that it's meaningless."

He went on. "Sometimes, the walls you're in, the ones you apparently feel like kicking down, are the very ones you put up yourself. Maybe that's the answer you're looking for."

He left before I could tell him it wasn't. "Sorry, professor," I yelled after him. "Not everything's a crappy metaphor." Somehow I got the energy to trudge down the stairs to grab the emergency lanterns, leaving a trail of plaster wherever I stepped, something I was sure Mrs. Harpton was not going to let me forget anytime soon. But the hole in the wall was large enough for me to crawl through now, and I was determined to see what was inside that secret room.

THE SECRET ROOM was apparently hiding mildew and mold. That was all I could smell as I stood in the darkness. I couldn't see a thing, even with the lanterns on, only tiny dust sprinkles dancing in the stream of light. My skin crawled in the thick, stagnant air as I thought about what else could be in here. Black widows, bats, Mrs. Harpton's rotting corpse from 1885, the one the house kept locked up in this hell hole so her ghost would have to clean twice a week.

But thankfully, and unfortunately, there was nothing. Nothing but bare walls and an empty room. I tried not to feel disappointed, like Geraldo Rivera right after blasting into Al Capone's vault after two hours of hyping it. But there was nothing here. "F-ing metaphors," I muttered under my breath.

I tried to let my mind be still. Maybe I could connect with the beings that were trapped in here. There had to be a reason this place was sealed and forgotten. I could picture where all the desks were, the children sitting with their perfect curls and slicked-back side parts.

"Hello," I said to the air. "You're free now. You can go."

A loud flapping sound, like wings, lots of wings, came straight for me. Screaming, screeching birds that sounded almost human. The lantern slipped from my hand and crashed to the floor. I could hear the back of the battery compartment falling off, batteries rolling somewhere around my feet. I didn't have time to search for them. The bird sound got louder, and I shielded my eyes and head because I've seen *The Birds* and that's pretty much the only defense strategy you need to remember in a bird attack. I didn't feel beaks pecking at my skull like I expected, only wind blowing from far away, so far away I could barely feel it.

I got up after a moment, realizing I was being crazy. I wasn't in danger after all. I was just hallucinating, which was one of the signs Rosalie told me to look out for from the channelings. A sign I probably needed a break from it all.

I ran my hands along the dusty planks of the floor where the batteries had fallen. It was too dark to see, but somehow I managed to pick them up and locate the spring in the battery compartment, popping them back in correctly. I turned the light on again, searching the empty room. Maybe Jackson was right. Maybe nothing was my answer. Empty, meaningless nothing. I made my way back over to the hole, light streaming through, guiding my way.

Something was stuck to the bottom of my shoe. I could just see the small, rectangular paper peeking out over the toes of my boot. I tugged it off and brought it out with me. A postcard.

THE HALLWAY SEEMED EERILY quiet as I turned the card over and over in my fingertips while sitting on a pile of wall.

The front of the card was very plain by today's standards, marked only by the words: Private Mailing Card addressed to Henry Bowman of Langley Street in Landover, WI. It didn't have a photo of a vacation resort or even a return address for that matter. I flipped it over.

May 4, 1901

Dear Mr. Bowman,

As I have told you before, you must not send for me again. I am not who you think I am, and if I come, you will no longer have a choice when I leave. Your fate will forever be sealed. Think of your own children, and their children's children. This deed shall cost thee all thou art worth. Do not choose this crooked mile.

It wasn't signed, but I could guess who it was from. Crooked mile, crooked man, a crooked stile. This was all very familiar, like a poem I'd heard somewhere but had long forgotten. I wiped the dust off my phone and punched it into the browser. It instantly came up, first search.

There was a crooked man, and he walked a crooked mile
He found a crooked sixpence upon a crooked stile
He bought a crooked cat, which caught a crooked mouse,
And they all lived together in a little crooked house

An old 19th century nursery rhyme that shouldn't have meant anything to me, yet my hand shook holding my phone as I read it. I was connected somehow. Henry Bowman had been a crooked man who walked a crooked mile. And we were definitely living together in a crooked house. But what did it mean?

I felt a twinge of guilt looking at the hole in the wall, the piles of dust and debris around me, and all for a postcard.

"At least Geraldo had been paid to bust into that vault," I said, kicking myself. Damn it. I needed that seance. And now I had a broken wall I needed to pay to fix.

I fanned myself with the postcard then read the words again: "I am not who you think I am."

Maybe, it was time I knew who I was too.

CHAPTER 13

NO PLACE LIKE HOME

*R*osalie slumped over her cash register, eyes barely focused when I said "good-bye" to her that Thursday. It had been a few days since I told her about our seance replacements, and she still hadn't snapped out of it.

I knew it wasn't about the money. A hundred dollars a piece wasn't anything. She was depressed because she'd thought she had the upper hand in the negotiations with Paula, and we'd been easily replaced.

I almost felt like I shouldn't leave her.

"You okay?"

"Fine."

"That's not a 'fine' people use when they really are fine," I said.

"I guess I just thought people liked us." She stared off at an empty hippie store. "The ladies at the country club... the rich people on the lake. Apparently, there's no difference between us and any other mediums."

"Why don't you come with me?" I said.

"Don't be ridiculous. I can't close up shop for a couple of days," she said, like business was booming. "Go. Your mom misses you."

I kissed her cheek and told her I'd call her every night to check on her, then I left.

Jackson appeared as soon as I turned my car on. "Well, that was dramatic," he said.

I stared at him a second before pulling out of the parking lot of the strip mall the Purple Pony was located in. "Who asked you to come?"

"Let's be honest with ourselves, shall we?" He looked out the window. "Today is Thursday, the day Mrs. Harpton inspects the house again. And there's still a three-foot pile of drywall sitting in the hallway. We both know that's why you're leaving."

I stared at the steering wheel. "And that's why you're leaving too, I suppose."

"Of course. I can't be around for that. No one has ever touched Gate House. I am not going to be around to find out what happens. Plus, I need a break from our houseguest. She was a suffragette, you know, not sure if you heard that yet. When are we returning?"

"Sunday. I don't want to be in town for the seance either."

He looked at me, his transparent beard almost fading into my dark upholstery. "Sunday. You got that much time off from the house?"

I didn't answer.

"You did put in a formal vacation request, didn't you?"

I sucked my lips in. "Should I turn around?"

"Just drive," he said. "I'm probably not returning at this point anyway. At least your mother doesn't talk nonstop about marching in a corset."

I ignored his sarcasm and told him all about the channeling and the case itself. We had a lot of time to kill, and even though I hated to admit it, I was glad to have the company on such a long drive out to Indianapolis.

"So Sir Walter lied to the police?" he said when I got to that part.

I nodded. "According to the report, he told them he lost his hat when Bessie begged him to come back. I didn't see the report myself, though. Paula has it. But, none of that happened. I know because I was there. Bessilyn didn't beg. He did. And he threw a wine glass out into the parking lot, not his hat."

"Interesting."

"I was going to confront him at the seance, but that's not happening now."

I looked off at the highway in front of us, trying to think of a way to still make that happen.

A ROOSTER WEATHERVANE creaked on its pole above my mother's red brick townhouse, making me realize just how perfect everything was at her place. From the dark green trimmed windows to the little black mailbox, it all screamed of my mother's motto in life: Don't touch anything; I just Windexed.

I wiped my sticky-with-Dr.-Pepper hands on my already-stained sweatshirt and tried to unlock the door but couldn't. I inspected the key, too tired for this. Too tired for anything, really. I'd just driven eight hours straight with my annoying ex-husband, and my body couldn't decide if it was having a caffeine rush or a nervous meltdown.

I knocked with one shaky hand while ringing the bell with the other.

Myrtle, my mother's tabby, hissed at me from behind the door.

"Geez, Louise. I'm a comin,'" said a woman's voice that was not my mother's. I almost checked the address even though this had been my home for all of my life outside of my marriage.

A woman in her 60s with unusually red hair flung the door open and gave me a large welcoming smile. My mother's friend

Brenda. She told me to come in out of the cold. It was close to 70 degrees outside.

The inside of my mother's house looked similar to the outside. No dust dared to sit on the drill sergeant's kitty cat knickknacks. No coffee cups meandered on random coasters, wondering if they were done being used for the day. Nothing but straight-off-the-showroom perfection allowed here.

"Marlene!" Brenda yelled toward the back of the townhouse. "Carly's here."

My mother waltzed into the living room like she was making an entrance in a Polident commercial: large smile, just the right amount of lipstick, and a bounce in her step.

She kissed both my cheeks. "Why'd you ring the bell?" she asked.

"My key doesn't work."

"Of course it does. We've only had the one key."

"Yes, I remember the day you finally gave me a copy when I was fifteen, after I swore on the Bible I would never lose it." I held it up. "And I haven't."

Brenda leaned in and whispered in her ear.

"Oh, that's right," my mother said, pushing a loose gray strand behind her ear. "Brenda lost her keys so we had the locks replaced."

I sat down on a perfectly fluffed, leather couch. "Brenda lost her key? Wait a second... Brenda has a key?"

My mother didn't let me finish. "The ladies will be here for some Hand-and-Foot in about half an hour. They're all excited to see you. I'm making sandwiches. You want tuna or chicken?"

"Tuna for me," I said. Hand-and-Foot was my mother's favorite canasta-type card game, and "the ladies" meant the group of retired women who got together once a week to brag about their children, and their grandchildren. I was already suspicious of my mother for hosting. She probably wanted me to hear first-hand what the competition was up to so I'd step up my game.

I opened the door that led down to the basement, lifting my rolling suitcase over the familiar orange-carpeted stairs. My mother followed me down. "I put a mattress down here for you, but let me know if it's too crowded. I've kind of set up shop down here."

What did that even mean? I peeked around the corner. It smelled like fresh paint and fabric. My jaw dropped. Three different kinds of sewing machines were sitting on tables with fabric hanging off of all of them. Large wooden, half-painted boards were propped along each of the walls except for one where, right next to the litter box, was an air mattress with a folded sheet set on it.

My mom was right behind me. "Isn't this great? I was asked to make costumes and set designs for the Christmas play this year. Gotta start early. It's a big job."

"You know how to sew?" I asked, mouth still open. My mother had been an engineer.

"It's really not that hard. All you have to do is follow a pattern."

I nodded. No wonder. Following a pattern was never my strong suit in life.

She continued. "I could set up something upstairs in my office, but I still do consulting for Stellaplex, and I have all sorts of files and things…"

I wheeled my suitcase around a rack of clothes. It dragged slowly through the shag carpet. "No, this is fine. It's fine. I'm only here two days, anyways."

Brenda called down the stairs after us. "Did your mom tell you about Gordon the dentist?"

I shot my mom a look. "Gordon the dentist?"

My mother dug one of her perfectly white Reeboks into the carpet. "Midwest Singles dot com. Brenda and I made you a profile after you called to say you were coming. It just makes sense. You seem lonely."

I ran a hand along my aching eyes.

"Do you want to see your profile? You're picking up lots of hits."

"Oh God no. I mean, maybe. I mean, no."

"Don't worry. We made sure to weed out the dodos. We put in that you were only seeking professionals. And absolutely no smokers."

"Sounds very selective," I said.

"I hope you don't mind that I made you dinner plans tonight with the dentist. We'll have dinner together tomorrow night." She looked me over. "You should probably clean up."

"I don't want to go out to dinner with a non-smoking professional tonight. I just drove eight hours and I'm tired." I sat down on the saggy air mattress, my butt touched the floor. She handed me her phone and I saw a dark-haired man laughing at a golf course.

"He plays golf," she said, pointing to the man.

"I see."

"Just like you."

"In high school. And I only joined the team because it was easy to get a letter." I flopped onto the mattress. I hated to admit it, but the dentist was cute, and I was, technically, desperate.

I scrolled over to my profile picture, a picture of me pretending that my root beer was alcohol with a group of friends from golf, in high school. "Speaking of high school, this photo is from high school."

"It is? No wonder I never see you in that cute blouse anymore."

"Yeah, because it was cute fourteen years ago." I handed her phone back. "Long walks by the lake? And it says here I'm a teacher. I'm not a teacher. This whole profile's a lie, and a cliche. And I don't need your help dating."

My mother headed back up the stairs, apparently finished with our conversation. She paused on a step and turned around.

"About the teaching part. It's not a lie. I looked into it. You already have a master's degree. If you joined an accelerated program, it would only take you another year to get your teaching credential," she said like I should be excited to hear I was only a year away from making her proud.

I knew my mother was just being my mother, a person who saw a logical solution to every problem. And, I had a lot of problems. I needed a better job, so I should go into an accelerated teaching program. I needed a boyfriend, so I should set up a dating profile.

Logic was ruining my life.

Jackson appeared by my side on the mattress as soon as she headed back up the stairs. He gestured around the basement at the props and sewing machines. "And they say you can't go home again."

"Shut up, " I whispered, very aware of how it would look if anyone noticed me talking to him. I left him hover-sitting on the mattress and went up the stairs after my mother. The queen of distractions wasn't going to get away that easily. Now was as good a time as any to ask her the many questions I came here to ask.

As I opened the basement door, I heard the ladies already there for cards. She was queen for a reason.

"Don't worry," Jackson said, appearing by my side again. "I'll merely be a fly on the wall when you go on your date. With a golfing dentist, I hear. My, my. I'm very impressed."

GORDON THE DENTIST had the kind of hair-to-head ratio that makes you stare, mesmerized by whether he had hair plugs or just oddly spaced follicles. He looked a lot different than his profile picture, but then so did I.

I pulled on the spaghetti straps of my halter dress, trying to minimize the amount of cleavage I was showing and took a sip of water, pretending to be interested in what the man was saying when the only thing I could think about was my mother. She hosted cards and sent me on this date on purpose, so I wouldn't have time to ask her about the adoption. She'd known all along. That sneaky woman was good.

Gordon set his menu down, folded his hands over it, and smiled. "So, you're a teacher. What's that like?"

I didn't see the fly on the wall yet, but I knew Jackson was here somewhere, laughing. I decided lying was easier than explaining how we came to this lie. "Teaching. It's just as rewarding as you'd think it'd be. Kids are the future, you know. And I help them get that way."

Gordon stared deeply into my eyes. "That's so authentic. I think so many people are fake nowadays. I truly believe the only way to find real love is to be authentic right from the beginning."

Stretching his arms across the table, he touched the tips of my fingers with his, and I held in the urge to scream. I wasn't expecting that kind of authenticity.

He lowered his voice. "I'm going to be super-authentic right now. I feel a connection with you I don't normally feel. What do you say we ditch this place and go for a ride? You wanna see my BMW? My house? I have a wine cellar." He winked.

And this is why you don't use party-girl profile pictures from high school...

I drew my hands away. "It's my turn to be super authentic with you, Gordon. I'm not really a teacher. I work retail at a hippie store and I live with my ex-husband."

His face dropped.

"He's dead. A ghost. I see ghosts all the time. I talk to them, too. They're some of my best friends, the most interesting and authentic people around. There are probably some here in this restaurant that will come out if we call them. Should we call them?"

He was right. Being authentic felt amazing.

Gordon's lip curled in a kind of concerned-yet-disgusted expression. He turned his head to the side. "If you weren't interested, you could just have told me. You didn't have to pretend to be weird. I prefer honest people."

An older woman appeared by his side. She had thinning gray hair and a thick face. "My Gordy-pie. He's a nice boy, but I don't approve of what he's doing. He can't pay for this dinner so he tries to get girls to leave with him before they bring the wine. He's a dentist, but he's got so much debt. I worry."

He got up to leave.

"Your mother doesn't approve of what you're doing here, Gordy-pie."

His face dropped. He threw his napkin onto the plate and looked all around the restaurant. "Wait, what? What did you call me?"

"Gordy-pie, your mother says hello. She also says you're a nice boy," I coughed on the word boy, and nice. "But you do this all the time. Leave before the wine is served because you can't afford it. She wants you to be truly authentic, by living within your means and being honest with yourself and others."

I was ad-libbing, and I was on a roll.

He practically fast walked into the waiter on his way out. I chugged my water and wiped my mouth with the fine cloth napkin in front of me. Maybe we all had disapproving mothers in life. Sir Walter's didn't approve of Bessie. Gordy-pie's hated his debt. And mine wanted me to be a teacher.

Jackson appeared on my way out. "I heard what you said back there about ghosts being the most interesting and authentic people you know."

"Don't flatter yourself. I only said that for shock value. Let's go," I said, not even caring that the restaurant was staring at me now. "It's time I dealt with my own sneaky and disapproving mother."

CHAPTER 14

DISTRACTIONS

*E*ven though I'd moved the litter box so it wasn't right by my head, I tossed and turned all night. The air mattress sunk and squished in weird ways whenever I turned, but that wasn't why I couldn't sleep. I hated confrontations with my mother.

My mother woke me at 8:00 for breakfast, but once I made it upstairs, I realized there was more to this than just eggs.

She handed me my agenda for the day, printed out and highlighted in two different colors. I sat at the breakfast bar and pretended to be impressed.

"You'll see, in yellow, that I made arrangements for you to talk to a counselor at eleven," she said, pointing to my schedule. "But, you'll need to leave here at ten to get there fifteen minutes early, which is just common courtesy."

She and Brenda were both in the kitchen. Brenda was frying eggs, humming to herself over the pan, looking right at home with an apron around her thick hips. I was just about to ask if she lived here when I replayed my mother's words in my head. "Wait. What kind of counselor are we talking about?"

"A career one."

"Is this about teaching?"

"Or editing. Or nursing. Or anything."

Brenda smiled up from the eggs. "Is this done enough for you, dear?"

I nodded. "Thanks, Brenda."

And there it was. The reminder that I wasn't good enough the way I was. At least there were professionals to help me be better at life. I folded the paper and stuffed it into my pajama pocket without looking at the rest.

My mother was already dressed in perfectly pressed jeans and a sweater, her short gray hair tucked behind her ears. She walked over to me. "Honey, I'm just worried you're not doing enough with your life, that's all. It goes by fast, believe me. You need to get out there and network, Xerox that old resume, go to job fairs and temp agencies..."

"Temp agencies?"

"And..." she said, pulling a small cardboard box out from under the breakfast bar. "I found these for you."

I took the box even though I was deathly afraid there might be a Rolodex and a pager in there. The box was lighter than I thought it'd be. I set it on the bar, and lifted the flaps as my mother smiled proudly on.

Peeking inside, I saw what looked like 20 overly thick, grayish white volleyball kneepads looking back.

"She spent all yesterday morning searching for those," her friend Brenda said from the stove.

I pulled one of the dingy white things out of the box and squished it between my fingertips. "What are they, anyway?"

"My old shoulder pads."

I dropped it back into the box.

"They'll make you look like a real dynamo in job interviews. We used to sew them into all our suit jackets, blouses too..."

I closed the box back up. I would've preferred the Rolodex, or anything that didn't involve 40 years of sweat stains.

"They've been washed," she said, probably because I was curling my lip, then added. "You can't find them this big anymore."

Was she seriously handing down a box of humungous shoulder pads like some sort of sad feminist baton, or was she trying to distract me with this gift of gross? She knew what I came here to ask. I blurted it out. "Mom, I don't want a box of your old shoulder pads. I mean, thanks, but I'm not taking those. Or career advice from the 80s."

She pursed her lips. "Most things stand the test of time."

"Not when those things are shoulder pads and the word dynamo. And I didn't come here for those. I want to see my adoption papers. I know this is hard, but it's time. I want to know names. If not my biological parents' names then the name of the adoption agency. I want to see the blanket you say I came in. I want to know everything you can tell me about who I am. Not who you think I should be."

Brenda handed me my plate of eggs and hustled out of the kitchen.

"Sit," my mother said, motioning toward her bright yellow kitchenette in the dining room. She sat down next to me. "Do you know how happy your grandmother was when I told her I was adopting you?" she asked, making me roll my eyes. Her first tactic of distraction hadn't worked, so now, just like always, she was moving on to plan-b. The emotional detour.

She continued. "Thrilled. She was thrilled. Not just because she couldn't wait for grandchildren but because she couldn't wait for me to experience the joys of motherhood too. And you were something else. A real handful. Curly blonde hair that was larger than life. I didn't know what to do with it."

I tugged on one of my curls. "Still don't," I said, kicking myself a little for getting sidetracked on the emotional detour with her.

"I thought I'd missed my chance to be a mother. Most adoption agencies wouldn't even let single moms apply back then. And I wasn't about to get married just to have kids."

I nodded. I decided to allow this detour, but only until I saw the telltale twitch. It was the little eye spasm that let me know when she wasn't telling the truth, or that she was hiding something.

"I was walking out of Stellaplex one day when one of the guys from legal stopped me. He told me his cousin was looking for a good home for a baby she couldn't take care of, and he knew I was looking to adopt. He said this young woman would essentially *give* me her baby if I complied with the terms. I couldn't comply fast enough. I'm still complying."

I knew what that was like. I had to do something similar for my free house. "The guy from legal, was he the lawyer for the adoption? What'd he look like?"

"Oh, I don't remember that," she said with an eye twitch.

I salted my eggs. "What did the couple look like? My birth parents?"

"Never met them." No eye twitch. She was telling the truth. "Never even saw a picture. The lawyer brought you here. We signed the paperwork right on this very table." She smoothed her hand over the dotted formica like she was picturing it. "You were so cute in your little purple blanket. I was ready to sign my life away when I saw you."

My mother didn't cry. But her voice cracked a little as she talked. "I was told if I didn't comply with the entire agreement, and it was a very thick agreement, I would forfeit my legal rights to you. I can't legally tell you anything more than that."

"But that's gotta be over, Mom. They can't take me away now."

She looked down at her hands. Her eye twitched and spasmed.

I decided to change gears. "What about the lawyer?" I said, mouth full of eggs. "Tell me what you can about that guy. He would be old, but he might still be around."

My phone rang and I pulled it out of my back pocket. It was Rosalie. "Hold on, Mom…"

My mother was still talking. "The only thing I remember about that man is the mustache" She chuckled. "And the pens. My goodness he had a lot of pens in his shirt pocket and this handle bar mustache that I think he waxed… looked like one of those western movies."

My jaw dropped. "Ohmygod, I *am* your free house," I yelled across the table.

"Carly," Rosalie said through the phone. Her voice was light, cheerful almost. "I need you back here ASAP. We're on for tomorrow's seance."

"W…what?"

"You heard me. Paula Henkel never changed the tickets to say we were no longer the mediums. That's why nobody cared it wasn't us anymore. They didn't know it wasn't us anymore. But when the ladies at the country club found out… Hooey! I heard they went bonkers. They fought for us, Carly."

"That's wonderful."

"We're getting half the basic ticket sales and anything extra we pick up like tarot-card readings. This is huge. This is huge."

I clicked off and hugged my mother. "Thanks for the information about the lawyer. Can't stay for the career counselor, though," I said. "I'm making the big bucks now."

My eye twitched a little.

CHAPTER 15

A NEW FOUND CONFIDENCE

*I*t was just a door now, like always, no signs of
destruction or repair. No sign that a crazy woman had
kicked her way into a secret room a couple days ago. I looked
high in the corner, right below the ornate doorframe where I'd
first seen the folded edge of wallpaper, painted over and begging
me to pull on it. There was nothing there now. And not one
crumb of drywall on the hallway floor either.

Only a letter taped to the outside of the mysterious door,
addressed to me:

> *Dear Ms. Taylor,*
>
> *This letter serves as a formal written reprimand of your attempted*
> *destruction of the property known as Gate House, as inspected by Mrs.*
> *Theona Harpton. The house agreement explicitly states no part of said*
> *property can be altered in any fashion. Please refrain from any more*
> *destructive attempts. After three formal reprimands, appropriate actions*
> *can be expected.*

I almost kissed it. It was confirmation that I was supposed to
have done that. I was figuring things out. Maybe. Once again, I

really had no idea. But, my actions that day should've warranted a lot more than a mere note. I most definitely got the impression this house had things to show me, if I was bold enough to find them.

I bolted down the stairs, a new found confidence and energy in my step. I had a clue about my adoption. The lawyer. I was about to solve Bessie's murder, and make a large chunk of money in the process. Maybe I could afford boots that didn't cut my circulation off, after all.

The morning sun streamed in through the window, and I heard talking in the kitchen. I quietly moved toward the conversation. "Oh good, you're awake," Jackson said when he saw me. I expected to see Bessie, but instead I saw the lawyer.

Ronald's stiff, tweed, gray suit seemed to impede his movement as he held his hand out for me to shake it. His jacket hung loosely open, revealing the unusual amount of pens in his shirt pocket. "Jackson told me you have some questions for me." His voice was very human, natural, with just a hint of a quiver.

"Yes. About my birth," I replied, unsure of how to approach the subject. "And my adoption." I hadn't expected to confront the lawyer so soon. I hadn't had time to prepare what I was going to say.

Tugging on the end of his mustache, he raised an eyebrow at me. "I can give you a lawyer's perspective if you have questions about the adoption process and your rights within it," he said, making his way over to the dining room table. He motioned for me to sit and he pulled out a chair and sat next to me, just like a regular human. I watched him with the same eagle eye I'd given Mrs. Harpton.

Jackson disappeared, leaving me to fend for myself.

"I have reason to believe you might know who my birth parents are," I said.

"Adoption documents are usually sealed unless you go through the proper channels."

The scrapbooks were laying on the table and I flipped through the first one until I found the photo of the classroom. "Why do you and Mrs. Harpton look like these people?"

He didn't answer.

I continued my interrogation. Even if he never said a word, at least I was getting it all off my chest. He would know that I knew. "My mother wouldn't tell me a thing about my adoption except what the lawyer who made her sign a six-inch-thick agreement looked just like you."

I studied his receding hairline for any traces of sweat, not that ghosts could sweat. There wasn't even a drop. I went on. "But how could that be? That agreement was signed thirty-one years ago. You would have been a child thirty-one years ago."

"I understand you are very emotional."

"That's not an answer. That's an observation."

"I'm very busy, and I do not have time to entertain this line of questioning. I have to fly out of here in ten minutes. But I can hear in your voice how important knowing about your biological parents is for you. If you have any questions about finding your biological family members, I am more than happy to assist."

After a few seconds of us raising eyebrows at one another, I finally gave in. "Okay, tell me what you can."

He basically gave me a helpful starter guide I could've found on a google search, including the many reasons why people don't want to be found and how both parties should respect that. So I already knew, without any documents or information, I was pretty much at the same crappy standstill as before.

At 5:00, Bessilyn and I passed under the glitter unicorn into the Purple Pony. Rosalie pointed to the cardboard box with moons on it marked *Seance Stuff* as soon as she heard the wind chimes on the door.

She was already pacing, her thick arms barely able to flail properly in the slightly too-tight, sleeveless (and shapeless) dress she loved to wear for seances. "It just burns my damn butt, that's all," she said, spit spraying a little as she talked. "I know that woman trashed my place, and she should pay for it, in addition to the seance."

"I thought a wild animal tore up your place."

"I rest my case." She motioned to the box I was carrying. "And we're bringing everything, the whole shebang... my candles. My crystal ball and EMF reader. My table cloth. That should all cost extra."

I put the box down. I could tell we were going to be a minute. "Well, we're over it," I said. "After tonight, we never have to see that woman again. Let's just make some money and be done."

I knew I needed to confide in Rosalie about the real reasons I was doing the seance, though. "I'm also going to figure out Bessie's killer tonight. I did a channeling with her last week..."

Rosalie studied my face, staring in my eyes. She didn't even bother to hold in her look of disappointment. "Why didn't you tell me you'd already done that? I would've checked for signs."

"I knew you'd worry. I'm fine. I don't think I've had any ill effects related to the channelings."

"No eyesight problems, odd behavior, or hallucinations?" she asked.

"I'm not possessed yet, if that's what you're asking." I didn't mention the fact I tore through a wall for no reason and heard bird sounds while I was doing it. "But there are still pieces to this puzzle that are missing. Sir Walter seems especially suspicious. He married a year after the party and he lied on the police report."

Bessie appeared by my side. "What are you talking about?"

I'd forgotten she hadn't known the Sir Walter stuff. She'd spent the rest of last week resting from our channeling session.

I spoke softly when I told her everything. I knew it would be hard for her to hear it, not just the part where Sir Walter had lied to police but also the fact he had married just a year after her death, and that he'd had kids.

Her face lost color and she stared at her feet. She hadn't known any of it.

"I can't go. I can't face this, or him. The seance is over," she said, fading into the rack of dresses behind her.

"We're very close to figuring out your murder. I can't do it alone."

Rosalie checked her watch, pretending not to stare at me talking to air. "I hate to interrupt," she said, pointing to the door. "But we're gonna be late."

I made one last ditch effort. "Bessie, you have to go to the seance," I said.

"What? She's not going? We signed a paper guaranteeing she'd be there." Rosalie snapped her fingers in the direction I was talking. "Bessilyn Hind, get in the car now."

"I don't think she's going," I said. "We're gonna have to fake it." As we were leaving, I added. "If you stay here, Bessie, then you're letting your murderer get away with murder once again."

I could only hope guilt still worked on the dead. But I had no confidence in that, not even the new-found kind.

CHAPTER 16

SHOW TIME

*R*osalie blinked her eyes at the dark living room of the bed and breakfast as she stood in the doorway, mouth open. It was almost as decadent as Bessie's birthday bash.

Buffet tables had been placed all across the sides of the spacious room. Waiters dashed this way and that, carrying trays, setting everything up. I smelled bacon somewhere.

"Welcome, welcome, welcome ladies," Paula said in her black leggings and matching witch dress, her spiky blonde hair sprayed with glitter. "I hope you approve."

Paula Henkel sure knew how to cater to her rich clientele. Deep purple and black velvet material had been draped across the ceiling of the dance floor, making the place look like a mystical circus. Cushy chairs with small tables were all around the outer perimeter so everyone could get a good look at the show.

And in the middle of the dance floor was what I knew would act as our seance table, the extra-long dining table covered in a glittery black cloth with a crystal ball, an EMF reader, some candles and tarot cards on it. Nine chairs were already placed around. I wondered if Rosalie had counted the "premium spots" like I had. There were supposed to be five. Paula was making extra money everywhere.

Rosalie looked nervously at the cardboard box I was still carrying with the word "seance stuff" scrawled across the front with a black sharpie. She bit her lip.

"I'll get rid of it," I said, knowing we weren't going to need Rosalie's threadbare black tablecloth or half-gone candlesticks after all. I scanned the place for somewhere to hide it, purposely asking the waiter who was setting up trays of bacon-wrapped, who-cares-so-long-as-they're-bacon things on one of the tables. I grabbed one. Then another. He threw me an annoyed look, extending his arms out to take the box I had just asked him to take.

"Don't worry. I'm one of the mediums," I said, like that meant extra bacon. "So, keep 'em coming." I grabbed another bacon thing as soon as he turned his back then hurried back over to Rosalie and Paula because they were arguing again.

"I never said half of gross. I said half of net," Paula said.

"I know you could not have said half of net because I would never have agreed to something so foolish. That's like agreeing to half of nothing."

Paula's smirk was as wide as her head as she strutted around Rosalie. "I see you're here. You must be agreeing to my terms."

Rosalie smirked back. "I see you've set up. Looks like you're agreeing to our terms, which is half of gross sales. I'd hate to see all of this go to waste."

"I can still call Dragon Fire and Emerald."

"Do it."

The ladies were pretty close to each other, Rosalie shaking a little on her bad hip as she bent down to Paula's level.

I stepped between them. "Paula, look. I think Rosalie can agree that this must've set you back quite a bit." Paula threw her hands on her hips and nodded her head so hard it looked like she wanted to free it from her neck.

I went on. "But I'm also sure that Paula, here, can agree that she can reuse much of this stuff on a second or even a third seance someday. Something Rosalie and I would be happy to do again, if we're treated fairly at this one..."

Both ladies seemed to calm down enough to negotiate, and I walked off.

Jackson appeared beside me, an almost transparent version of himself in front of one of the large windows. He blended almost seamlessly into the curtains. Thankfully, I remembered other people were here or I might've started talking to nothing again. I was getting way too comfortable having conversations with ghosts.

"You look especially beautiful tonight. Gordy-pie is missing out," he said, making me roll my eyes and smooth out my black sweater and skinny jeans.

He scanned the room. "Has Bessie seen the displays yet?"

I looked around before whispering into the curtain. "She's not coming. If you'd have bothered to show up earlier, you could maybe have helped me talk her into it."

"Let me remind you; I am a new apparition. When I ride on the living, I have to do it in low energy mode. She's much more experienced."

"She decided to stay at the Purple Pony." I whispered out of the side of my mouth to the curtains beside me.

"You told her about Sir Walter, didn't you?"

I nodded, almost forgetting to whisper now. "But only because she had a right to know."

I looked out the window at the parking lot where, not too long ago, horses and "motor cars" had been lined up around lanterns.

Poor Bessilyn. Apparently, love wasn't any easier to handle after death.

Rosalie and Paula had ditched their scowls and had their client-smiles back on by the time dinner and cocktail hour had rolled around. They both greeted one perfectly manicured older woman in a thousand-dollar black outfit after another, just like they were besties at a slumber party.

Christine's mother-in-law was there, a woman in her 70s with a tanned, "still enjoys the lake" face and a skeptical smile. She introduced herself as Amelia. "I've been a member of the women's club for fifty years," she said. "I've never seen anyone do more for a member." I didn't tell her I wasn't doing this because Bessilyn had been a founding member of the women's club in its early years. I couldn't tell anyone the truth about why I was doing this. I hardly knew myself.

But I did know pretty much my whole paying audience consisted of women's club members, so I played it up like that was why we were all here.

When I was alone, I stared at Bessie's display, noticing the description had been altered to question if she'd been murdered, and I gulped, wondering how I was going to figure things out without her being here.

"She was beautiful," someone said behind me, a shaky, frail hand pointing to Bessie's portrait photo next to the description that began "*A Suffragist With a Heart.*" I turned.

"Technically, I wasn't invited to the cocktail hour," Mrs Nebitt said, raising a glass of wine at me.

"I won't tell a soul," I replied. "But you let me know if you need a refill. I happen to know the crazy medium working tonight."

She looked lovely in her pale blue dress, fluffy white hair in curls. "Are you ready?"

Just having someone ask me such a question made my stomach flop. "Every time I turn around, more and more people come in." I was nervous, but I was also getting better at doing seances too. The first one I'd done months ago with Rosalie had been a dud. Shelby Winehouse's fiancé told me as much. I hadn't charged for that one, but I was pretty sure he was close to asking for his gas money back.

And honestly, I could see why the mediums of yesteryear used vaudeville tricks in their seances, making tables shake or pretending to levitate by jumping at the right moment. It was incredibly hard to make the dead seem interesting if you didn't jazz things up a bit. Without props and extras, seances were a lot like having a pretend friend. The other people in the room could do little more than watch you talk to yourself. So now, I always made a point to narrate every side of the conversation I was having with a ghost and I always asked the ghost to show their presence by moving something or flicking the lights. Something any ghost, no matter their power level, could usually handle.

Paula Henkel plowed through the crowd like a first responder in a crisis, carrying a Ziploc bag with a disintegrating yellowish orange folded paper in it.

"Mrs. Nebitt," she said, turning her attention to the librarian beside me. "I'm so glad you could come, and you're early too. Complimentary guests aren't supposed to arrive until 9:00." Paula's eyes drifted down to the librarian's glass. "Enjoying your cocktail?" She over-enunciated every syllable.

"I'm trying," the woman said, downing her wine, making me like her even more. "It's a little dry. One might even say it's 'unpleasantly bitter'. I'm going to find the waiter to see if you have beer." She waddled off.

"Be sure to try the bacon-wrapped things," I called after her. "They're delicious."

Paula pushed her lips together, holding the plastic bag high in the air so it was in front of my face. "You're paying for her."

I cocked my head to the side. "You know, it's the strangest thing. I'm suddenly feeling ill. I think I should go home."

Paula's lips drained of their color. "This seance had better be good," she said through clenched teeth. "Or there won't be a next time."

"It will be good," I said. "But next time, the five complimentary guests you invite from town will be invited to the dinner and cocktail hour too. We treat our locals like family around here, even if they're family we don't always like. Got it? Now is that Sir Walter's police report?"

I went to snatch the bag, but Paula pulled it back. "Wash your hands before you open this, and no food or drink. I'm probably going to add all of this to Sir Walter's display case soon. I'm only giving it to you so you can confront Sir Walter with the information tonight." She handed it to me. "In other words, make it look real."

Jackson, who had been snickering off to the side the whole time, followed me over to a lit table in the back.

"Paula has been going around telling people not to talk to the *main medium* until showtime," he said. "Now I know it's because she thinks you're full of parlor tricks and that you'll accidentally give the strings away."

"Doesn't surprise me," I said, a little too loudly, then looked around to see if anyone was watching me talk to myself. I wiped my hands on my black skinny jeans and opened the bag.

The paper was fragile. It felt almost like a thin breakable silk. The writing was almost too faded to read, done in a ridiculously loopy kind of cursive. Jackson read over my shoulder.

"I told you Walter's suspicious," I whispered under my breath to the ghost sitting next to me. "This is not the way it happened that night. He's lying, and I'm going to confront him with it."

"Oh, good plan," my ex-husband said in his trademark snotty tone. "I can hardly wait to hear you explain to a room full of honored guests how you absolutely know Sir Walter was lying in this police report from more than 100 years ago because you were there that night, taking notes."

"I'll make it work somehow. And you'd better make an appearance if this thing gets dull. I don't think Bessie's showing up. And I can't guarantee Sir Walter's even here. So, flick the lights, rattle some chains or something."

"That's a little too trite for an English professor, don't you think? And where would I find chains last minute, anyway?"

I looked up. Rosalie motioned for me to join her at the main seance table. I folded the paper up and tucked it back into the bag. "Show time."

Everyone's eyes were already on me as I made my way across what used to be the dance floor, secretly glad Paula had forbidden anyone from talking to me during cocktail hour. The whole place went quiet. I could hear every click of my still-too-tight boots, clunking along the wooden dance floor.

Paula didn't look at me. She gently set a large glass fish bowl full of tickets on the table.

"I found out they paid $30 per raffle ticket," Rosalie said in my ear, nodding like I should do something about it. "And we know that's all extra. I'm so mad I could cuss."

"Don't," I said. "Our reputation's on the line and she's not worth ruining it for. Not even one *damn*. These ladies are not that kind of audience."

I couldn't help staring at the bowl Paula was currently swishing her hand around in, trying to guess how many raffle tickets were swirling around with it, trying to times everything by $30. I stopped myself and took a deep breath.

Stop caring about petty "living" problems. You have a ghost to cook here.

"Put your mics on," Paula instructed, pointing to the clip-on kind that news crews always wore. My hands fumbled like they'd forgotten how to work. Things were too ritzy for me. There was too much pressure…

Paula smiled at the close to one hundred people in the crowd, her white-blonde hair shimmering in the dim lights over the dance floor, like a spiky disco ball. "All right," she said. Her voice echoed over her mic and the applause died down. "Who's ready to have a good time? We have three premium spots. This first one is the best. The person will be sitting right between our two mediums so they'll be able to see all the action up close, maybe keep these ladies honest," she laughed. "Doubtful. And this very enviable spot goes to..." She pulled out a name. "Caleb Bowman."

"Oh shit," I said into my mic.

CHAPTER 17

STRINGS ATTACHED

The room was dark except for the dim spotlight hitting the table and the candles lit around us. I tried to look at Rosalie before we started, but Caleb was in the middle of us and he stuck his face in the way, bugging his beady eyes at me, making them almost look normal sized. He whispered so low my mic couldn't pick it up. "I am going to expose you for the fraud you are. Better hope I don't see you moving this table."

My heart raced, but not as fast as Caleb probably wanted it to.

"I've done some extensive research for tonight's seance," I began into my mic, trying to keep my voice low and mystical. "This lobby, the exact spot where we're sitting at right now, was the main room of Bessilyn Margaret Hind's birthday party. Just upstairs was where she died. Was it suicide or was it murder? That's what we will find out tonight."

"It was suicide," Caleb said, this time loud enough for the mics to pick up. "I read the police report myself."

"Oh, Sheriff Bowman. You of all people should know the police in Landover County don't always know what they're talking about," I said, playing to the audience, who laughed right where I wanted them to.

I opened the Ziploc and carefully laid the paper out on the table. "I have the exact police report right here that we will be asking Sir Walter Timbre about. In case you don't know, he was Bessilyn Hind's fiancee just before her death, and the heir to Crown Frozen Vegetables. This paper may prove he is also a liar." Little old ladies in the back craned their necks to get a better look.

"It will be on display soon," Paula chimed into her mic from her spot at the table. "I'll keep you all posted, just sign up for my newsletter."

Seances were different than a channeling in a lot of ways. Channeling was a ghost taking over your body. Seances were you nagging whatever ghosts were in the room to have a conversation with you, whether they wanted to or not. You never knew who was going to show up, or if they were going to be angry about being conjured. You might get a ghost who'd ridden in on a human that night, or you could get the ghosts haunting the place you were doing the seance in. Those were the ones I was going after, at least at first. I'd probably end with all that sentimental "Mom loved it when you wore her pearls to Hamilton" garbage.

I picked up one of the items Paula had placed on the table, a metal bell hanging from a loop that was on a stand. "This is a spirit bell," I said, holding it up, almost rolling my eyes. She'd certainly done her homework. The bell was usually a parlor trick, though, an easy way for mediums of old to ring when the lights were off in an attempt to trick their audience. "Spirits sometimes ring a bell when they want their presence known. Tonight, we are hoping to conjure up as many guests from Bessie's birthday party in 1906 as we can. I have heard the Landover Bed and Breakfast is haunted by many. If you noticed the two display cases, those are the two we will try to talk to first."

I led the group in a breathing exercise, which was really just for show, and then asked for Sir Walter. "Please make your presence known. We welcome you here as a member of our party."

After a few moments, the spirit bell clanged loud and clear, and a gasp fell over the crowd. Jackson was sprawled across the table, flicking it. "I couldn't resist," he said, his head resting on his hand.

I ignored him. "Yes, yes. A lot of energy here... Sir Walter, is that you? I'd like to ask you about the night of Bessilyn Hind's death."

Nothing happened, except for Caleb chuckling to my left.

"Sir Walter," I added, trying to make the ghost angry. An angry ghost was a communicating one. "I know your police report is nothing but lies," I said. "And I implore you to come to the table and defend yourself."

The table shook, the candles flickered, one spilled over, its wax running across the tablecloth, dangerously close to the police report. I snatched the paper up before anything could happen to it. "You'd like that, wouldn't you?" I said. "Trying to get rid of the words you said that night. I'm guessing because I was right when I said they were a lie and Bessie hasn't seen them yet. Let me read straight from the police report so Bessie knows what I'm talking about. She's here too, you know?"

That was the part I was probably going to have to fake. Bessie's response. No biggie, though. I was there that night. I knew everything that Bessie would probably say. Sir Walter would know I was lying about her being here, though, but no one else would.

I coughed, pulling the paper up to one of the candles so I could see it better, but not so close Sir Walter could burn it.

"The witness's account as he remembers it exactly on that day: Sir Walter Timbre, 40, heir to Crown Vegetables, last saw the deceased at her birthday celebration at approximately 9:00 on the night of Friday, September 14, 1906.

"Mr. Timbre says it was at this time when the two engaged in a heated argument, whereby Miss Hind ran into the woods and Mr.

Timbre followed. She begged him not to call off the wedding, but he did not comply. Miss Hind then took his hat and threw it into the woods. Mr. Timbre promptly left the party. When asked why he attended the party in the first place, he responded that the deceased had begged him to come.

"Shortly thereafter, Miss Hind was found in her room with a self-inflicted gunshot wound to her heart. The door was locked and there was no sign of entry."

A loud crash rang through the room as all three of the large windows in the back of the lobby blew out at once; glass shattered and clanked onto the porch in the front. The audience screamed as a cool night breeze blew around us now. I thought I saw Caleb Bowman's face grow deathly white. The bell was next. It rang at first then shot across the room, swooping just above the patrons' heads in the crowd. It hit the back wall, clanging to the floor somewhere.

"Lies," Bessie said. "Come out and show yourself, you coward."

I breathed a sigh of relief. She did come. Yay for guilt.

I repeated Bessie's words back to the crowd, and I heard a couple of women say, "You go, girl" in response.

She went on, shouting at her ex-fiancé. "Did you really tell the police in an official statement that I begged you not to end our engagement? I begged you! No wonder I get no respect as a women's rights leader!"

I felt his presence before I saw him. "Walter's here," I told the crowd. They gasped.

"Bess, I've waited so long to talk to you about this."

"Oh really," she said, incredulously. "Then why have you been hiding from me for years when I call to you?"

Walter looked different than he had at Bessilyn's birthday party. He was older and thicker, but still handsome. "The police officer said those things. I merely agreed."

Sir Walter was a strong ghost, but meek. I could tell by how colorful and lifelike he seemed, hovering over toward Bessie. I filled the audience in on what was going on and they all swooned when I described Sir Walter because I still emphasized the handsome parts.

"You were my true love," he said. I repeated it.

"Then why on earth did you kill me? And remarry the next year..."

My audience was all on the edge of their seats. The lovers' spat. The murder. It was my best stuff.

"No. No," he said. "The report is a little bit of a lie, sure. I was merely saving face over what happened that night, but I didn't... I couldn't... You killed yourself. We heard the gunshot."

"I'm sure *you* heard the gunshot. You were the one pulling the trigger." Bessie liked to throw stuff when she was angry. A wine glass this time.

"Bessie," I said, and I knew she could hear me. "I'll have to end this session if it looks like you're going to hurt someone. This is a safe setting for you two to have your argument."

The audience booed me. Even though a cool autumn breeze was blowing through the broken windows at this point, apparently, the audience wanted more destruction.

I looked over at Paula. Her eyes were wide, round almost. She looked from one side of the room to the next then back again, like a dazed animal.

Bessilyn continued. "After our argument where *you* begged *me* to come back to you, saying all sorts of lies about how you didn't care what other people thought... you snuck around the back of my house, up to my room where you murdered me with my own gun. Your hat was never tossed into the woods. It dropped when you dropped it there."

"I can assure you, Bessie, I did not. I would never hurt you."

"Poppycock!" Bessilyn lifted the table. It levitated for a second before tilting. The police report fell into her hands before I could say anything. Then it floated in midair above the crowd. They screamed and gasped, craning their necks to see if there were strings. Caleb stood up, stumbling into someone's table as he followed the paper across the room, eyes fixed on it. He grabbed it from Bessilyn who snatched it back.

Sir Walter was silent. I knew he hadn't left, though. I could still feel his energy.

When I heard him again, his voice was lower, sadder. "After our argument, I wanted to say something to you in the woods to comfort you. You looked so beautiful leaning against that tree. But pride wouldn't let me at that point," he said. "And you went back inside. I stewed in my anger for a long time, just sitting in my car, wondering what to do next. That's when I noticed people sneaking around the side of your house. They seemed to be running from one window to the next, actually. So I went to investigate."

An audience member screamed out "bullshit" when I told them this. *Maybe the ladies club was that kind of an audience.*

He went on. "Two young women, dressed in party clothes. They were giggling by an open window to the kitchen. Your friends…"

"Kate and Agnes! They did show up. I knew they would," she said, her voice trailing off.

"I confronted them, in a good-natured way, of course. I knew they were your friends from the Suffragist Society, and I wanted to help them surprise you. I wanted there to be something good about your birthday for you. We laughed and talked for a while. I was just convincing them to come inside the proper way, and not through the window, when we heard the shot."

I looked out at the audience, to the many red, watery eyes.

He continued. "We ran inside, and in my haste, I lost my hat. We were devastated like everyone else to learn what had happened. That you took your own life. That's what we all believed at the time. That you took your life, not because of me. But because, somehow, you weren't allowed to live the life you were meant to live. We had that struggle in common. Both of us caught in family businesses. I loved you more than words will ever express."

He hovered closer to Bessie as he spoke. She could easily have moved away, but she didn't. She probably knew he couldn't get too close, anyway.

"This is the part I didn't want to tell you. Kate and I consoled each other, and a year later, I realized I could love again, and we married. But that doesn't mean I didn't also love you."

"I will never believe it," she said.

"My parents were the ones who encouraged me to end our engagement. I found out later it wasn't really because of your age. It was because they were hoping your parents would be angry enough to end the business deal if we broke up."

I gasped through my microphone then filled everyone in on what was going on.

He continued. "The cannery was in jeopardy of closing. Your family was going bankrupt. The only way out of the deal was to have your parents demand it."

"Lies," Bessilyn shouted then disappeared and, after about 10 seconds, so did Walter. I could tell they were done. I folded my arms onto the table and rested my head into them, exhausted. I still felt a presence. A smaller, but stronger, one. One very eager to be heard. And one I recognized immediately from my channeling. Martha. I was pretty sure of it.

I blew it off, shooting back to the present when I heard the applause. A standing ovation.

"You didn't solve any murders," Caleb said, "because there weren't any murders. It was a suicide."

"I guess this story will have to be continued," I said in my mic to more applause.

"And now," Rosalie said. "Who wants to see if a dearly departed loved one came to see them today?"

A wind circled through the broken windows as Paula glared around the room at the mess she had to clean up, that was going to cost a fortune. I had a feeling, along with Bessie's murder, our seance agreement hadn't exactly been solved yet either.

CHAPTER 18

HONORED GUESTS

I skipped down the stairs the next afternoon, my mind still reeling with the clues from the night of the seance, more certain than ever that Martha held some real information, not just about Henry and Eliza and their meet-up in the bathroom, but also about who killed Bessie. Martha saw something the night of Bessie's death, just after she handed her the washcloth to put over her eyes. I heard it that night when she stumbled over her words, and I was determined to find out what that was.

There were three messages on my machine.

The first one was slow and shaky. "Hello. This is Mrs. Nebitt. I just wanted to tell you what a wonderful time I had last night at the seance. I'll never know how you did it, windows breaking, paper floating across the room. Wonderful performance. I talked to my friend Mildred. You know Mildred Blueberg, the woman who wrote the book I was telling you about," the librarian said, like there were hundreds of Mildreds running around. "We're meeting…" Beep.

The answering machine cut her off and moved to the next

message. It was Mrs. Nebitt again. "I am not a fan of technology. Anyway, if you are so inclined, Mildred is at the library now if you would like to come by. As you know, she is only here for the summer. So, hello? Hello? Did this thing cut me off again?" Beep.

I was certain now the third message was going to be the librarian again. I actually couldn't wait to meet Mildred. I had a very important question to ask her about running retractions on thousands of self-published books.

But the next message was Rosalie. "I'm gonna kill that woman. You know what she said? She said we had to pay for damages." She sighed heavily into the recording. "I'm about to show her what damages really are."

Rosalie was still pretty upset when I called her back.

"A thousand bucks. One thousand dollars for each window. And you'll never guess who that sparkly troll wants to pay for them."

It took me a minute to understand what my boss was talking about. "Wait. What? But we didn't break those windows. Bessie did. I have no control over what ghosts do at a seance. I'm so glad we added that into the agreement." I stroked my dog's short golden fur as I talked. He looked up at me with his soft brown eyes, the cute little V-shaped scar on his nose. I knew the agreement was ironclad, too. Jackson had his attorney write it up, which was the least that attorney could do for me, considering all I knew about him.

"She thinks you broke out the windows on purpose as part of your show. And she says all elements of your show should've been disclosed in the agreement before she signed it."

"I'm sure her insurance will pay for it. We'll split the deductible."

My head hurt and just about every part of my body ached for some reason. Who knew seances were so draining? The last thing I wanted was to talk business right now. "I have to admit," I said, reliving the moment in my head. "Those windows were my favorite part."

"Paula Henkel's face when that happened was priceless... Like a money balloon being popped." Rosalie chuckled. "I'm telling you, though. I can't handle her anymore."

"I'll go over there today," I said, mostly because I wanted to talk to Martha.

"I'll go with you," Rosalie said. "I don't trust money balloons. They try to re-inflate to new levels."

"Good. I want to try to talk another one of the ghosts haunting the bed and breakfast into coming back to Gate House with me, to do a channeling." I mumbled that last part, mostly because I knew she wouldn't approve. "So I need a distraction."

"Your distraction?" she said. "More like your enabler."

I hung up and headed over to the library where I found Mrs. Nebitt in the periodicals section, sitting with two other older women behind the microfilm machine. I recognized the one in bright blue with her long gray hair swept up in a beautiful bun as Delilah Scott. The other woman had bright purple stretchy pants, a naturally yellowed smile, and a sensible short white haircut. She stood to shake my hand when I came over and I realized she couldn't have been taller than a fourth grader.

"We were just looking up some articles for Delilah," Mrs. Nebitt said, quickly leaning forward. She flicked off the microfilm machine before I could see what they'd been researching, making me wonder why. "She heard a growling noise a couple of weeks ago. The police came over and basically did nothing..."

Mildred interrupted with a gruff, confident voice I almost wasn't expecting. "And they only did that much because she's a Donovan."

"Only by blood," she said.

I nodded. I knew that she was a Donovan, one of the founding members of the town and the country club. She was like Potter

Grove royalty. But she was about twentieth in line for the throne, and that was her problem.

"I don't think the police believe me about the growling." Her voice was low with a quiet, velvety kind of confidence I noticed rich people often had. "I've heard it twice since then, and Caleb hasn't done a thing about it. But then, he's a Bowman, and the Bowmans have long thought I'm a bit crazy. I'm still sane enough to know it's the other way around, though." Her soft blue silk scarf matched her eye color perfectly. "Sorry, dear, I know you're a Bowman."

"Just by marriage."

"Ah, isn't that the best kind of family? The one you can divorce."

I almost told her that wasn't always the case, at least not if your dead ex-husband decided to haunt you.

I told them about how Rosalie's shop had been ransacked the other day, and how the incidents were probably related.

"Probably," Mrs. Nebitt said. The other ladies looked at her like they didn't think so.

I pulled my chair over to them, a loud squeaking noise came with it, but Mrs. Nebitt somehow held in her shushing. Mildred leaned into me as soon as I sat down. "Debbie tells me you're trying to solve an old murder," she said, making me smile because I finally knew Mrs. Nebitt's first name.

I nodded. "Yes, thank you, Debbie, for filling everyone in." Debbie shot me a look like I should never call her Debbie again. I continued. "I don't think Bessilyn Hind committed suicide. I tried to figure it out during the seance the other night, but I haven't quite got it."

"Yes, we all heard about that seance. It's the talk of the library," Delilah said, dismissively.

"Thanks," I said, even though I wasn't sure that was a compliment. "So, what were you ladies looking up?" I leaned forward toward the microfilm machine, eyeing the power button. Mrs.

Nebitt watched my every move and cut me off at the pass by putting her hand on mine. "Carly, here, did a fantastic job. Best medium I've ever seen."

"How many mediums have you seen?" Mildred scoffed.

Delilah Scott smoothed her scarf along her shoulders with a trembling hand. "Debbie hasn't talked about anything else. It must have been wonderful."

"Oh, you bet it was." Mrs. Nebitt looked at the ceiling like she was remembering it. "You should have been there. The bed and breakfast went all out for the ladies at the country club. Paula Henkel said it cost a fortune, and then the windows blew out."

"I don't think it cost that much," I added. "Paula exaggerates, especially about those windows."

Mildred put her hand on my shoulder. "Bessilyn Hind, huh? I did a whole write-up about her in my book."

I sat forward. Now was my chance to ask her about retractions. "I'm glad you brought that up. I'm very close to figuring out her death. It wasn't a suicide, though. That much I know for sure."

"Really?"

I looked down. "I can't prove it yet. But when I do, would you be willing to include an addendum or possibly even a retraction in your book?"

Mildred laughed so hysterically she had to grab the desk so she wouldn't fall over. "I am not reprinting anything. Horace would kill me if I added even one more book to the book fortress we still have in the garage."

"What if I took all the books you have and added the retraction as a sticker?"

"Take the books?" she said in disbelief.

I nodded.

"And you'll do all the work?"

"Plus, maybe we could have you do a signing on the updated version, help you sell a few copies," I added.

Her face lit up. "You had me at take the books. Horace is gonna die. But still, I'm only okaying this idea if Bessilyn's death is officially changed."

"Like I said before, I'm very close to figuring it out. There are just some loose ends that don't make sense and a couple more people to interview."

They looked at me like I was crazy.

I turned to Delilah. I was getting used to crazy stares. "You've lived here a long time. Do you remember the Timbre family or the Hinds?"

Delilah threw a fragile-looking hand over her chest. "Am I one of the people being interviewed? I don't know much about either family, sorry. I am old, but not that old."

Before any of us could do the math, she added. "I only knew of the Timbres and the Hinds. Both families kept to themselves. But I did hear it was Bessie's parents' car accident that brought out the news that the Hinds were not doing very well. There was hardly enough money for a decent funeral. And, years later, Pleasant and her husband ended up selling the cannery too, for dirt cheap, to the Timbres, I believe."

"Oh my goodness," Mrs. Nebitt said, her voice trembling a little. "This is exactly what Sir Walter said last night at the seance. His story checks out. And there is no way Carly could have known those details. She is, by far, the best medium I've ever seen."

"And I thought we were finally going to talk about something other than that seance you were invited to," Delilah said, glaring at Mrs. Nebitt.

"I told you to buy a ticket, Delilah," Mrs. Nebitt replied. "And come with me."

"I can't stay up that late, anyway."

Mildred leaned into me. "Why Delilah Scott wasn't considered an honored guest we'll never know."

Mrs. Nebitt's attention went to her fingernails, and I saw my chance.

"So," I said, reaching over to turn the microfilm machine on before the librarian could stop me. "What were you looking up about the growling..." I stopped mid-sentence as my attention went up to the monitor in front of me.

"We learned they're back," Mildred said.

Mrs. Nebitt shushed her.

CHAPTER 19

THEY'RE BACK

nother Bird Attack in Landover. That was the title of the article from 1954 we were all staring at on the screen. And I had to admit, I was not expecting birds.

"I remember it like it was yesterday," Delilah Scott said. "This wasn't the only attack."

"Nope," Mildred replied. "Not by a long shot."

I quickly scanned the article. In it, a young woman recounted an attack by crows on her way home from secretarial school when she tried to take a short cut through the woods.

Bertha Hawthorne, nineteen years old of Landover, narrowly escaped injury today after she says birds attacked her near the country club during the annual Independence Day water ski show.

"I only took the shortcut because I didn't want to miss the show. I heard growling first. Then, when I looked up in the trees, they came at me like bombs. Birds. Some were bigger than I've ever seen. Probably about twenty of them. Good thing I had my book bag. I swatted them away until this dog came out of nowhere and rescued me. He's a regular hero, like the allies in Normandy," she said.

There was a photo of Bertha, a petite brunette girl in a perfectly pleated skirt, squatting down by the dog the paper had dubbed "Normandy." My eyes bugged. The dog looked just like Rex, only this dog's nose was bandaged.

"This marked the beginning of the crow years," Mildred said like I would know what that meant.

"They weren't crows. I've never heard of a crow that looked like that," Mrs. Nebitt interrupted. "They say it was a fluke. Mutant birds crazed with some sort of flu, descending on Landover Lake because they were searching for water in their crazed state. That's all. We need to forget about it. They're not back."

Delilah wrung her tiny, wrinkled hands together. "They were awful. Angry, greasy, black birds with beaks that looked like fungus-infested toenails, thick and yellowed. They would lurk in the trees."

"Lurk," Mildred agreed.

Mrs. Nebitt shook her head. "It only seemed that way. They were searching for water."

Mildred went on. "You couldn't see them, but they could see you. Waiting, watching."

"I was a young mother at the time," Delilah said. "With three kids. Terrified. Those birds would watch some people and do nothing. But then, suddenly, they'd choose someone, and it was awful. Just awful. They'd attack, one right after the other like little bombs."

"It seemed like they had an agenda, selectively killing people," Mildred added.

I realized I was holding my breath, and I exhaled. "C'mon. Did anyone actually die? These are birds we're talking about."

"Oh yeah," Mildred said, matter-of-factly. "Those beaks could penetrate a skull. Horrible when you think about it. And almost unpreventable. How many times do you notice birds?"

"I'll be noticing them a lot now, thanks," I said. "In my shiny new helmet."

Mildred ran her finger along the words and the picture on the screen. "Nobody knows why those awful things chose Landover County or how they selected their victims, but after about two years, they left. Poof, like that." She snapped her sausage-like fingers to indicate just how quickly they had killed and gone.

"Do you think it's related to the shapeshifters here?" I asked.

Mrs. Nebitt made a dismissive gesture. "I hope you don't give in to those sorts of notions." She gave the other women a hard stare. "Those are just rumors. There is no evidence of shapeshifters anywhere, and I am a highly trained researcher who likes to believe the experts in life."

Mildred turned toward her longtime friend. "Then, highly trained researcher, explain why these experts hid how many deaths there were? There's not a count anywhere. And other than this article, there's hardly any coverage. This is the only article I know of that mentions the growling."

"If I remember correctly, there was a lengthy article about the mutant birds…"

"Only after so many people were outraged there wasn't any coverage about them," Delilah said. "I'm pretty sure the growling I've been hearing is the same one we all heard back then with those birds. So, you see, I doubt this is what ransacked the Purple Pony."

I chill ran up my arm. I looked at my phone. It was getting late and I needed to meet Rosalie at the bed and breakfast soon. "Can I have a printout of this article, please?" I asked, getting up to leave.

I knew it must just have been a coincidence. A lot of dogs looked like my dog, a golden Labrador with especially dark sensitive eyes and a bandage where my dog now had a scar…

"Twenty-five cents a copy," Mrs. Nebitt replied.

I opened my purse and searched the bottom for some change, which reminded me just how desperately I needed to get paid for that seance.

CHAPTER 20

JUST A RUMOR

J couldn't help but picture the parking lot at the bed and breakfast just as it had been the night of Bessie's party. The horses and carriages. The motor cars that didn't look too different from their horse-drawn counterparts. A large part of me needed to go back. I needed to feel the solid wooden floorboards clunking under my narrow 1906 boots. The itchy, stifling clothing, the bowler hats on the men. I was going to talk Martha into doing a channeling with me. I wasn't sure how. But I needed to do another one. And not just for clues.

The evening air was still hot enough to be summer even though the trees were changing into their yellow and orange autumn hues; the full moon seemed extra large this evening. A gentle breeze blew through my hair, bringing with it the smell of Paula's garden, the sounds of rustling leaves… and a soft growling. I looked up at the branches overhead, searching for whatever animal had made the sound, wishing I'd actually bought that helmet.

I was pretty sure the noise had come from the opposite side of the house and, even though I knew I shouldn't go after it, something also told me I had to. This was where I'd heard the same noise a few weeks ago, when Paula suddenly appeared carrying wood.

Clinging to the side of the house, ready to bolt at any moment, I peeked around the corner. Across the yard, over by the begonias, stood what looked like a large brown bear twitching wildly in the bushes, hunching over like it was in pain, flailing its neck back and forth. It turned and our eyes met. Its face wasn't a bear's face. It had the delicate features of a human's mixed with a bear's.

Gasping, I pulled my head back toward the wall, but it was too late. Whatever that was, and I was pretty sure I knew what that was, had seen me. I peeked back over. It was gone, making me wonder, once again, if I'd been hallucinating.

My heart raced. The face had seemed familiar, but I wasn't sure at all who it was. I rushed back to leave, almost plowing right into my boss who was limping behind me. "There you are," she said when she saw me. "You ready?" she asked.

My mind still raced a little from the thing I'd just seen on the side of the house, but I managed to nod out a yes.

"You sure? You don't look so good."

"I'm sure."

Do I tell her?

We walked toward the house, and I kept looking around the yard, wondering where the shapeshifter went. Some things, even after you've heard they exist and are fully expecting to see them someday, still almost make you pee your pants when you actually see them.

"Just so you know, I'm not being nice to Paula," Rosalie said as we approached the front door. She was dressed in her black pantsuit, the one she called her power suit because it gave her instant confidence. I almost offered her a pair of shoulder pads from the box I had in the back of my car.

"Just stick to the script," I said. Somehow I had talked Rosalie into negotiating with the dreadful woman while I tried to find

Martha and talk her into going back to Gate House for a channeling.

Paula answered the door with a smile that quickly faded when she saw it was us standing there. "I heard you were ready to compromise."

"I heard *you* were ready to compromise," Rosalie shot back.

I elbowed my boss and she forced her mouth into something that showed teeth. "Yes, we're ready."

"Good. Because I've already ironed out the details. Ninety percent of the windows here at the bed and breakfast are original to the house itself. Replacing the glass is not a cheap endeavor..."

I moved toward the door. "And while you two look over the numbers from our seance and *negotiate*, I want to take some photos of the display cases... for my book, if you don't mind me including the bed and breakfast in there."

"What book?" she asked. "I don't know anything about a book."

"I'm writing a book about all the spirits I encounter from my seances. I'm calling it The Ghosts of Landover. I was hoping to feature the bed and breakfast in it. Give it a whole chapter with a detailed account of the seance too."

Free publicity seemed to soften the woman up a little, just as I'd hoped it would. She motioned around the room. "Take as many photos as you'd like. Now's actually a good time. Most the guests are off at dinner or watching the sunset at the lake." She motioned for Rosalie to follow her into the small office behind the front desk. "But if you think that chapter means you don't have to pay for windows, you're sadly mistaken."

Jackson appeared beside me when they left, and I almost jumped like I saw a shapeshifter. "Awww, I still take your breath away," he said. "That's sweet. You would do that for me too, if I had breath anymore."

I lowered my voice. "Did you ride in with me just now?"

"Yes."

"Then you must've seen the shapeshifter," I said.

He shook his head. "Like I told you before, Carly doll. Low-energy mode. I haven't sensed anything until now. But it sounds like I missed something amazing. A shapeshifter, really? But then, it is a full moon."

I scrunched my face up. "It wasn't a werewolf."

"Like they're the only ones compelled to shift during a full moon." He looked around. "You should just do the channeling here," he said. "I'm sure Martha has enough energy. The other ghosts don't even know she's around. If a ghost has enough energy to keep herself hidden, she's got plenty."

"Yeah, not happening. I don't think I can do a channeling anywhere but at home."

"So, you're prudish about that as well, huh? Do you need the doors locked and the lights out too?"

"Please just go."

He sat down on the red floral sofa. "I bet a lot of people have done a lot worse than channelings here, probably right here on this very sofa." He mocked a shocked face.

I ignored the pervert I used to be married to and took a picture of the display case in front of me. "Martha," I whispered. "You here?" The flash ruined the picture, so I took another one while shooing my ex away. "Go away, Jackson. I think you're scaring her."

He disappeared. Maybe he had a point. I could make the channeling a quickie. Tell her to begin right as she was coming up the stairs that night to check on Bessie and end when the police arrived. That couldn't have been more than fifteen minutes. There was no sense in dragging her to Gate House for it.

"Martha," I said again, taking another photo of the greasy driving glove sitting on the rock. I checked the photo on my cell phone. None of these were book-worthy shots, but I kept snapping away. A faint transparent image of a dark dress with a white apron showed up in the flash when I took my last image, which was something I hadn't expected. She was here, all right, but afraid to show herself. "Martha," I said. "I know you're here." I took another photo, seeing her again in the flash.

I whispered. "I need to know what you know from the night of Bessie's murder. I'm still not 100 percent sure about Walter. I'd like to do a channeling with you. A quick one. Fifteen minutes, tops."

She was small and transparent when she materialized almost thirty seconds later. Her face was expressionless, same saggy eyes, same sweet, trusting smile. She'd been a good friend to Bessie. Like a mom. I could tell.

"Her parents were never the same after Bessie's death," she whispered. "And honestly, neither was I. I came back here after I passed because this feels the most like home for me. But I don't want the others to know I'm here. They change things too much for me, and I just want to be quiet and comfortable."

I nodded like I understood, but death was a very different part of life for me. So I could only be understanding to a point.

"You probably heard at the seance that Bessie didn't commit suicide," I said. "I need to see through your memories if the murderer was waiting in Bessie's room for her that night."

"I don't think I saw anyone."

"Bessie didn't see anyone either, but I... I just want to make sure," I said. "I need another perspective."

"I don't know." Her voice was extra quaky. "If you think my memories will help, I'll do it but... I'd rather not relive it."

I didn't tell her that I wanted access to her memories for more than Bessie and her murder, that I also had my own selfish reasons. The Henry and Eliza bathroom moment. The fact I was drawn to channelings now...

Martha squeezed the tip of her almost invisible apron with her faded hands, wrapping it around each of her fingers. "Missy's been so angry, and I can't bear to see her like this. She needs to move on, stop holding in the hate from her life."

"That's where you can help. We have to hurry. Paula thinks we're here to negotiate, so fifteen minutes is about all we have. They'll be finishing their meeting soon."

The lobby smelled like autumn, mostly from the cinnamon and apple scent coming from the aroma diffuser on the mantle. Paula had already begun adding gourd displays here and there even though it wasn't October yet. I sat down on one of the flowered couches and leaned back into a red velvet throw pillow. "I'd like you to take me to the night of Bessilyn's death, the part when you went up to check on her."

I closed my eyes and tried to look like I was sleeping. That way, if anyone came in, I wouldn't look too strange. Not that I cared too much anyway. The only people who stayed at the bed and breakfast were vacationers I'd never see again.

She hovered nervously next to me, her voice was like a whisper carried on wind. "I didn't know what was happening downstairs. I was told by Mrs. Hind to straighten the upstairs bathroom and spare rooms where some of the guests would be spending the night. That's what I was doing when I saw Miss Bessilyn run to her room in a tizzy. And I knew that girl. When she got like that, the only thing she wanted was some warm milk and her pills."

My eyes bulged. "Perfect. That's right where I want you to start. Right then, when you saw Bessie running up the stairs."

"If you think it'll help," she said, looking around.

I nodded even though my heart raced too. I'd never done a channeling in public before. "Whenever you're ready," I said, trying to relax and let my mind think of anything but the shapeshifter I just saw or the negotiations being shouted out in Paula's office.

After a minute, the smell of apples and cinnamon from the bed and breakfast was replaced with some sort of lemon cleaner, and I felt myself humming. Voices rose in the background and they weren't Paula and Rosalie's. A man yelled, "At least Pleasant's married."

"You can open your eyes now," Martha said to me. We were in a room I didn't recognize, dusting under a lamp, humming as we went. A full-sized bed of dark mahogany with a white quilt beautifully accented the dark green leafed wallpaper pattern, making me wonder just how much canned yams cost in the early 1900s.

I could tell Martha was drowning out the sounds of the party. And she was good at it. She poured some more cleaner onto her rag and dusted along the bed rails. I concentrated on the sounds from downstairs while Martha tucked in the bedspread and fluffed up the pillow. I knew Bessie would be heading up the stairs soon. .

"Folks, let's hear it for my wife's pathetic, spinster sister," a muffled, slurred voice said from downstairs, followed by the loud sounds of plates hitting the floor, along with gasps, giggles, and screams of horror. I knew it was more than plates, an entire three-tiered cake.

Martha rushed to the door and peeked out into the hallway just as Bessilyn flew up the stairs in a beautiful champagne-colored blur, and I got to see just how strikingly gorgeous the woman had been, her high cheekbones and pointed little nose, soft light brown hair. I caught a glimpse of Eliza addressing Bessilyn as Martha closed the door again.

Martha's voice was calm as she spoke to me. "I didn't want her to see me. She was very upset. This is 'round about the time when I thought I should go downstairs and get her some milk and her pills. Miss Bessilyn had had a rough year. And now she was having a rough birthday too."

She stepped back and examined the room before she left, scanning over the dresser, the bed, and mirror. The Oriental rug was bunched up along one of its corners and she hustled over and straightened it up then darted swiftly out of the room and down the stairs.

Martha didn't even glance over at the living room and the party as she passed through. She scurried into the kitchen and went for the kettle. She whispered to me inside her head, commenting on the action. "That kettle. It was already full of warmed milk. I remember thinking that was odd 'cause usually I'm the one warming it, but it was the perfect temperature, and everything."

She turned, looking around. A younger housekeeper in a bonnet held Troy junior, the three-year-old sailor, along her hip while Troy's older brother ran around her, pulling at her apron strings. Martha ducked down while she poured the milk.

"That's Esther," she said, pointing to the other housekeeper. "I didn't want her to see me. Poor thing was given the children to watch that night once their grandparents left, probably why there was already warm milk," she chuckled. "I'm sure she was trying to get them to calm down, go to sleep, already. If she saw me, she would've wanted me to take a turn watching those monsters, and that wasn't neither of our jobs."

After pouring just a little milk in a cup, she hurried back upstairs again. She looked over at Bessie's room. "I don't go in yet," she said. "I remembered Mrs. Hind specifically told me to check the bathroom every half an hour and put fresh towels in there, and I hadn't done it even once yet, the whole night. Wish I hadn't checked it now. This part's a little embarrassing."

Martha set the milk on one of the linen closet's shelves, just under a wooden box on the top shelf with medicine bottles of varying sizes and colors. I wondered if one of them was chloroform.

"What are those little bottles on the top shelf?" I asked her.

"Oh, I never messed with those. They were Mr. Hind's, left-over from when he used to practice medicine."

"He was a doctor?"

"Until his father got too old and talked him into taking over the cannery."

Martha grabbed a stack of stiff white towels then headed down the hall toward the bathroom.

This was it, the part I personally couldn't wait for. Opening the door, I saw them only briefly. Henry Bowman had Eliza pinned up against one of the walls. She wasn't smiling, but she wasn't moving to get away either.

"I want you gone," he said. "You're no longer welcome here. You're a curse."

Her voice sounded just like mine. "This did not come without warning. Surely you remember me telling you to change your path or it would be the worse for you. Now, it's too late. You're knee deep in it. This deed of thine shall cost thee all thou art worth. You, your children, your children's children and all who aid you on your quest..."

They looked up and saw Martha. "Sorry," Martha said, putting her head down and closing the door.

"I couldn't wait to tell missy about that one," she said to me, as she shuffled over to the linen closet to put the towels back. She took the milk and shut the cabinet door. "Most people in town had a story or two about Henry Bowman and the lady he sent for from New York, and now we did too. He wanted that lady gone. She was refusing. And threatening his children. Who'd of thought that of a nanny?" Her voice lowered. "I didn't get a chance to tell missy the story, though."

She knocked lightly on Bessie's door. "You okay, missy?" she asked. "You want some warm milk? And your special pills for sleeping?"

The door creaked when she opened it. "I can't tell you," she said to me, "how many times I wished that I'd have stayed in this room with Bessie. That I'd have taken that gun. That maybe I'd have noticed more."

CHAPTER 21

THE OTHER SIDE

*M*artha went on and on, chattering to me in her head nervously. "I took care of Bessie ever since that girl was a baby, just a round little pudgy thing with rolls up and down her legs and a smile that reached from one ear to the other. I felt like she was my own kid. She wanted to leave her parents many times, live on her own. I was glad they talked her into staying time and time again. I would've hated living here without her. She was the only thing good about the house." She paused, her voice lowered. "I know that's silly to think that way. I was just the housekeeper."

"I'm sorry. I didn't realize what a hard memory this is for you to relive," I told her.

Martha peeked into the room. "Oh honey," she said, immediately running to the suffragette when she saw her eyes were red and swollen.

I looked around the room while Martha talked to Bessie about Sir Walter and the break-up. The armoire was open, the gun sitting on the top shelf, the window closed. I didn't see any signs of a person lurking in the shadows, waiting to kill Bessie as soon as her pills had set in.

But then, the bedroom was pretty messy, not nearly as spotless as it probably should have been with a housekeeper around, something I hadn't noticed as Bessie, but now, as Martha, I was noticing. Big time. You could hardly see the chair by the vanity because a heap of dresses had been strewn over the back, and they were not tiny dresses. Long billowy fabric that seemed to ball into a mess of fluff and lace.

Martha's eyes scanned the room as she rambled on about how she hated birthdays too, mostly noticing the mess she'd have to clean up later. Shoes and books took up a lot of the floor. I noticed a bunch of clothes under the bed too.

"I guess you know what happened downstairs," Bessie said. "Sorry for making such a mess with the cake. I'm too old for that."

"I was upstairs when it happened, but don't worry, miss. It wasn't your fault."

"Yes, it was. I shoved Troy into the cake."

"I could hardly believe that one," the housekeeper said to me in her head. "And boy, was I sure sad I'd missed it. That Troy was nothing but trouble. Mean as a mad dog. He had that shove comin,' and a few more, to boot. I always liked gossiping with Bessie about it. I tried to tell her a bit of my own gossip that night, but I could tell she was too tired to hear it."

Bessie's head rested on the backboard of the bed, her longish golden brown hair spilling out along her shoulders, her eyes half-closed.

"I'll tell you later, missy," the housekeeper said, kissing the top of Bessie's head. "You sure you don't want me to help you out of your party clothes?"

"Not yet. I'm starving, Martha. I didn't eat a bite all night."

"I told you that corset was too tight."

"Stop lecturing me, and be a dear. See if you can bring me a plate. And look around to see if Sir Walter's still here."

"Now I see why you're keeping your dress on." Martha walked

across the room to a pitcher on the dresser at the connecting wall. She poured water onto one of the soft white cloths stacked up to the side of the basin then handed it to Bessie.

"You rest your eyes. I'll... I'll..." Martha's voice trailed off. She pulled a small blanket from under the bed, picking something up with it: a dark pair of men's pants and a suit jacket. "What in the..." She put them back down on top of what looked like clean, tan driving gloves.

The glove wasn't from a distraught guest after all!

"What is it?" Bessie asked, pulling the cloth off her eyes and sitting up.

"Nothing," Martha said, smiling. "I'll see what I can bring you. I only hope I can do it without Esther seeing me. Your sister has her watching those devil kids of hers, and I know that poor girl's looking for me to relieve her."

Martha closed the door and headed downstairs.

"Did you recognize the pants and jacket?"

"Of course I did," she said. "I've only been doing the washing around here for longer than Bessie'd been livin'. They were her father's."

"Why didn't you ask her about them?"

"I didn't want to know the answer. Most women who acted like Miss Bessilyn, you know, driving fast and marching in them marches, they were also known to wear men's clothes at times. They were different. A lot of people already talked about missy like that, and I just thought I shouldn't be one of them, is all. She didn't need to feel different everywhere."

Martha moved fast for a woman close to 60, her bones ached and cracked after each step down the stairs, pain shooting through her knees, but it didn't slow her down one bit.

Downstairs now, I looked around the party to see who was there and could possibly have an alibi, and who was not. But Martha wasn't interested in the guests as much as I was. Her gaze went to the cake mess all over the floor, the toppled wine glasses, the spills and stains. She took a second to admire the mess, smiling at the two waiters who were busy cleaning it up. They didn't smile back. They threw Martha the evil eye like she should have been helping. "They were hired help just for the party, not family," she said, like she was family. "They didn't know what a joyous mess that was."

The other housekeeper I now knew as Esther ran up to Martha when she saw her, her blonde bangs had fallen out of her bonnet, cake smeared all along her dress. She handed Troy junior over to her. He smelled awful along our hip, like he needed changing, bathing, and maybe some of that lemon cleaner.

"Your turn," she said, taking a breath. "I'd rather clean up cake, thank you." She hustled off toward the hall. "But first, I've got bags and coats to fetch. Half the guests are leaving. Mrs. Hind is apologizing all over the place," she said. "Bessie sure knows how to end a party fast." She smiled and winked after that last remark.

Troy junior fidgeted to escape Martha's grasp, kicking the side of her thigh harder and harder, making her knees ache even more. She clutched him tighter and he burped, the smell of salami and milk rising up with it. I almost threw up. She put him down and he toddled over to where his brother and sister were dripping candle wax into a blob on the tablecloth. "Good riddance. Not my job anyway," Martha said.

Bessie's father, James, approached us as we searched the room for food to bring to Bessie. "Martha, is she upstairs?" he asked.

Martha nodded. "Resting."

"Good," he said. "She's not a girl anymore. Yet, she acts like one, right down to the tantrums. Probably because we treat her like one."

Martha just nodded. I looked around at the guests out of the corner of Martha's eye.

"Don't bring her a thing to eat. Do you hear me? She doesn't deserve to eat…"

That's when we heard it. The sound I knew was coming. It

was loud, no mistaking it. Louder than I thought it'd be. The sound of a gun. Bessie's life, ending. The final moment.

The band stopped. The room filled with screams so loud they echoed off the walls. Bessie's father's face drained of its color. The front door swung open and the guests who were in the process of leaving were suddenly back. Loud chaos ensued.

"Everyone okay?"

"It sounded like a gunshot," Troy said, staggering across the dance floor, his uniform still full of cake.

Henry Bowman bolted down the stairs. "I believe it came from one of the rooms," he said.

Bessie's father exchanged a worried look first with Henry then with Martha. He darted up the stairs, with Martha and several guests at his heels. He tried to turn the knob but it was locked. "Bessilyn Margaret Hind, open this door," he yelled, pounding on it, fist over fist. He threw his weight hard against the door, but bounced back.

"Let me try," Henry said. He was more than a head taller than James, a lot broader too.

"It's my fault," James said, looking at Henry, his eyes filled with tears. "I was warned. We were warned... The curse. Henry, the curse."

"Not now," Henry said, throwing his weight against the dark, heavy door.

It was at this moment that I finally recognized James, with his head lowered, and his eyes looking up. He'd been one of the men with Henry in the desk-dancing Eliza photo.

"Not Bessie. Not Bessie. Not missy. Please no..." Martha said, over and over as someone shook and tugged on her shoulders. On my shoulders.

"I think she's having a stroke," a voice said. "Carly, dear."

"Stop filming, Bobby. This isn't funny."

"It is from my end."

I recognized one of the voices. Rosalie. I blinked, my head

throbbing, my eyes not focusing right. It felt like my tongue was about six inches too wide for my mouth.

"Oh yeah. Drool away, baby," the man's voice said. My eyes focused. Rosalie, Paula, Shelby, and Bobby all stood around me. Bobby had a cell phone about two inches from my face.

Shelby scooted by him. "Are you okay?" she asked.

I nodded. "Just channeling," I said, still dazed.

Bobby chuckled. "I don't know what that means, but it was awesome. Totally made up for the boring seance I came all the way out to Gate House for. I thought we might need an exorcist over here."

"Oh, Bobby, shush," Shelby said, stroking my hair. "You're gonna ruin our anniversary."

He ignored her. "You were doing all sorts of voices. Low-pitched ones, 'Open this door,'" he said lowering his voice, mocking me. "And a high-pitched shaky one, 'Not missy. Oh no...'"

"Great," I said, kicking myself for being so public. I looked around, remembering where I was, that it wasn't 1906 anymore.

I shook myself out of my stupor, taking out my phone so I could jot everything down from the channeling into my notes app, as I wiped a little drool from my lip. I knew the information wouldn't last long. "This was your surprise anniversary gift?" I asked, furiously typing everything I could think of. "A stay-cation?"

Shelby nodded. "One year since he proposed," she said, holding out her hand to show off a dainty ring with a tiny blue stone. "He even got my mom to watch all the kids, all five of them including the baby and everything. More romantic than anyone thought."

"I re-proposed," Bobby said, proudly. "I got down on one knee this time, surprised her at the diner. I told her I'd do it every year."

I didn't bother to tell them engagement anniversaries weren't a thing.

Paula smiled. "I gave them quite a deal. A lovebird special."

"Special?" Rosalie rolled her eyes. "You should check your credit card. That means she charged you double," she said, making me realize she and Paula probably hadn't negotiated anything about the seance while I was channeling. But they both dutifully admired Shelby's ring, "oohing and aahing" at just the right moments while Bobby sat on the couch next to me and replayed his video over and over again, probably making a boomerang-looping gif with my drool moment.

That's when it came to me. The bear's face.

I leaned over to him. "You need to delete that video, Smoky," I whispered.

"Excuse me?" he asked, eyebrow raised.

I stared at him, the same way I had when we exchanged looks outside, when he was shifting forms. "Does Shelby know?"

"I'm afraid I don't know what you're talking about," he said. "But if you have something crazy to say, that wouldn't surprise me. Crazy people often talk about crazy things." He patted his phone like the video was proof of that.

I leaned in so close one of my curls brushed his shoulder. "She has a right to know, regardless of you deleting that video," I said. "And you know it. You and Shelby have a child together, for crying out loud. He could be a shape…"

Bobby handed me his phone. "Delete it. She needs to know, but I'll tell her later, on my own terms. Got it?"

I nodded, snatching the phone before he could change his mind. The last thing Youtube needed was a drooling video of me doing weird voices. Shelby looked over and nodded her approval, sauntering across the living room, her black and white rockabilly dress swishing out in all directions. She gave Bobby a huge lipstick-smeared kiss on the cheek.

"What was that for?" he asked.

"We are on a romantic weekend, and you are earning all sorts of brownie points," she said, running her hand down his cheek. "That was real sweet of you to let Carly Mae delete that video."

"Yep," I said, scrolling into his "recently deleted" folder to make sure everything was gone for good and couldn't be recovered. "He's a regular teddy bear."

I glanced over at the glove on display. There was no doubt it was the one under the bed. The murderer had placed it there along with a change of clothes. *A disguise to look like Mr. Hind?*

My gaze went from the glove to the dress and back again, my heart suddenly racing as an idea came over me. "I'd like to borrow the evidence from the display cases, please."

Everyone stared at me.

"I'm not one-hundred-percent sure who murdered Bessilyn Hind yet, but I can prove it wasn't a suicide. Can I borrow some things?"

"I charge a fee for borrowing my displays," Paula said.

CHAPTER 22

HARD EVIDENCE

*T*he full moon lit the way as Rosalie and I walked through the parking lot just before 9:00 that night. I couldn't help but wonder how many shapeshifters were out tonight, besides Bobby. How many there were in Potter Grove, for that matter.

She stopped and lowered her voice as soon as we were far enough away from the house that no one could hear us. "You weren't you back there. Your eyes were half rolled into your head. You were doing voices I didn't know you could make. If I hadn't shook you out of that trance, they would've called the paramedics. They were close to doing that."

I looked down at my $10 boots. They were either breaking in or I was getting used to the numbness. Probably the latter. I was getting used to a lot of weird things lately.

She continued. "You can't channel anymore. That, whatever that was, it couldn't have been safe and it certainly wasn't normal."

"I gave up on normal years ago," I said, smiling at her. She didn't smile back. "I'm very close to figuring out Bessilyn Hind's murder. I wouldn't have gone through that if I wasn't close."

"But, is it worth it?" she asked.

I didn't answer, and we both walked in silence. I knew she didn't understand why solving a 100-year-old murder was important. I didn't understand it too much myself, but I'd grown to like Bessie. I thought of her as my friend now.

I went on. "Look, I had to get that evidence. Bessie's window somehow didn't latch right. That's why it was locked when the police checked it. Or at least I think. And when I channeled with the housekeeper back there, I found out there was a pair of pants, a jacket, and those gloves under Bessie's bed. Her father's. Her murder was premeditated and calculated. Whoever it was wanted it to look like her father."

Rosalie gasped. "So, who did it?"

"I have my suspicions, but if I'm going to prove this to the police, I've got to link the evidence to the murderer."

"So, that's why you sold us out for a box of junk. So you could look it over better? Good to know your priorities."

She didn't give me a chance to reply. "But did you really have to say we'd pay half the damn damages? She signed a waiver saying we weren't responsible for damages. And she didn't pay for half of my damn damages when she trashed my place." She yelled toward the house.

"I thought a wild animal did that," I said.

"I'm not saying I know how she did it."

Rosalie was really dragging her leg while she walked. Something that happened when she got upset, that and the Tourette-like cussing.

She wasn't done. "I don't think we'll see dime-one from that seance anymore. Not now that she's been given the green light to fudge the numbers on those million-dollar windows."

I ignored my friend and listened to my boots clunking along the gravel for a minute. Their rhythm seemed almost poetic. I took a deep breath and closed my eyes, allowing the cool night air to chill into my lungs. One breath after another.

As a ghost, Jackson always said that life is wasted on the living. Probably because it's so easy to get caught up in petty squabbles when you're in the middle of life, like money or politics or gossip. "I can't believe he did this" or "she needs to pay for that" kind of stuff. The kind of stuff that consumes you and makes you forget just how good it feels to take a deep breath or listen to the sound of your own boots clanking along through gravel. The living moments.

"Damn it, Carly. I can't believe you agreed to that. At least we didn't sign anything," she said, under her breath. I was pretty sure me picking up the evidence tomorrow was the same as me saying that we agreed to Paula's terms, but I didn't mention that to Rosalie. Instead, I opened the door and held my arm out so she could use it as leverage to slide herself into the driver's seat.

I knew she didn't really need my help. It was just one of those living moments.

I watched her drive off then headed back toward the house to check out the one piece of evidence I was hoping still existed after more than 100 years. I had a good shot since ninety percent of them were original to the house.

I STARED up at the moon a second. It had been bright the night of Bessilyn's death in 1906 too. The murderer probably had no problems getting down from Bessie's window. I only hoped I wouldn't have any problems getting up. I needed to see how the latch worked, to see if my theory was even possible. I took a deep breath.

Was I really about to possibly kill myself to help a woman who'd been dead for more than 100 years?

The decorative rock jutted out in almost perfect foot and hand holds, plus there was a trellis too, but I didn't trust that. It looked even less sturdy than the ladder in Henry Bowman's library. Pulling myself up the first couple of foot holds, I tried not to look down. I wasn't even that high off the ground yet, but my lip still quivered and it wasn't just from the wind.

When I was almost to the window, I thought I heard voices and I stopped dead in my tracks. It sounded like someone taking a stroll, maybe. How on earth was I going to explain scaling the bed and breakfast's wall?

I grabbed the trellis and prayed it would hold my weight as an older couple passed just underneath me hand in hand, leaning into each other. The man had a blanket in his free hand, the woman a picnic basket, probably filled with the kind of stuff they both pretended to like in their dating profiles. "Late-night strolls with wine and cheese at the bed and breakfast..." I almost wanted them to notice me. Then, I'd yell down like a crazy person that he was probably a creeper with debt problems and she wasn't really a teacher.

They never looked up, never yelled that there was a crazy stalker climbing the wall, which made me realize this trellis was at a perfect angle, enough in the shadows not to be seen, and still pretty sturdy.

I continued up as soon as the couple had passed me. The thick Victorian-era curtains were closed on the inside of what used to be Bessie's room. I had no idea if anyone was on the other side of the window, though. I would need to be quick. And quiet. Just check the mechanisms of the latch then scurry down before anyone saw.

Even in the light of the full moon, things were too dark to see. I stopped myself from reaching for the flashlight on my phone, reminding myself that beacons of light were attention-drawing, and therefore, life-threatening at this point. And instead, I studied the dark window, willing my eyes to adjust to the dim lighting.

It appeared to be lifted just a crack, and under the crack, was a thin metal bar protruding out like a bit of a clothes hanger. I tugged on it and the latch moved. It worked. I tried it again, and someone screamed from the other side of the window, but the latch closed. My heart dropped, almost as fast as I bolted back down that trellis. The lights in the room came on and a male voice asked what in the hell was going on, but I was already down and running.

I took off into the parking lot. I really needed better plans in life. Any plans, actually. I kicked myself, realizing I probably should've stayed around for that career counselor, after all.

But at least I could prove for certain the escape route the murderer had taken, and why the police hadn't noticed anything. And I hadn't killed myself doing it.

Sitting in my car, I tried to breathe normally again. My hand shook as I turned on the heat, pulled out my phone, and brought up the pictures of the evidence I was planning to take over to the police department tomorrow, as soon as I picked it up from Paula.

Paula was only letting me borrow "certain pieces:" the gloves, the gun, and the witness accounts. I wasn't allowed to take the dress because, apparently, steaming out the wrinkles in a murder victim's gown and pinning it to a mannequin had been pretty costly. And in return for her generosity, the Purple Pony agreed to take half the net profit, something Rosalie was not at all happy about.

But with the glove alone, I could prove Bessie hadn't committed suicide. And that was probably enough to get her death certificate changed and the case reopened.

My phone rang. It was a number I didn't recognize, but I still answered it.

"Carly Mae? This is Mildred. I know I said I wasn't going to get the man's hopes up, but they're up. Horace wants these books out by tomorrow afternoon because we're leaving town soon. The lake house is only our summer home."

"Perfect," I said. "I think I'm about to get Bessie's death certificate changed." I was lying. I had no idea how hard that was going to be, and no idea what I was up against.

CHAPTER 23

THEN AND NOW

"I love it when the lake's like glass," Mildred said the next day when I came to pick up the books. We were standing in her backyard, staring off at the water, which didn't have many ripples disturbing it.

I clicked another photo on my phone. The dark water, the cloudy sky, the million-dollar backdrop. It was gorgeous. No wonder rich people paid so much to live here.

Mildred pointed across the lake. "You can't see it from here, but the country club's just behind that bend," she said, a gentle breeze blowing her soft white curls. Her property was one of the smaller houses along Landover Lake. There were only a few charming older ones left, most having been knocked down for fifty-story mansions. At the end of her backyard, where it met the water, was a lopsided dock with two boats: a pontoon, and a small speed boat.

A family of ducks quacked off in the distance, and I had to remind myself I had nothing to fear. Those were ducks, not skull-crushing, mutant crows. "Tell me why you think the birds are back," I said, my gaze darting all around.

"Delilah's not the only one who's heard them. I have too," she said.

I looked at her. "How do you know it was them? And not some other animal?"

"They don't sound like other animals, certainly not other birds. They make an almost growling noise that seems a little human sounding, if you wanna know the truth."

I actually wasn't sure I did.

She looked around and lowered her voice. "I was in Potter Grove at the Bait 'N Breath last week with my great grandchildren getting stuff to go fishing. Horace and I both heard it. A chill went straight up my spine and we hustled those kids back in the car faster than his pacemaker probably liked. And when I looked up, I thought I saw one in the branches. They like the high branches, so you can't see 'em as much."

The Bait 'N Breath was right next to the Purple Pony.

I must've looked terrified because she quickly changed the subject. "Just keep your eyes and ears open, and you'll be fine. Thanks for taking my books." She looked down at her dark sandals. "You sure you want 'em? There's probably more than a thousand left."

I coughed on nothing. "Yes," I said, even though I hadn't thought about the amount yet. "Don't worry, I won't do anything until Bessilyn's death certificate has officially been changed. But I'm close to getting that done, and I made a promise to her..." I stopped myself before I sounded like the crazy lady who makes promises to ghosts. People knew I did seances, but a lot of them thought I used sleight of hand and magic-trick gimmicks. Admitting I was friends with ghosts was going to put me on a whole new level of crazy for many people.

"You promised who?" she asked, leaning into me like we were old friends, and she wasn't about to let me get away with not telling her. I didn't answer. She grabbed my arm and continued.

"My dad was the caretaker at Landover Country Club when I was growing up. Did you know that? Sometimes he'd take me into work and some of the rich ladies there would feel sorry for me and pay me a quarter to help them out to their cars with their golf clubs and bags and things. They'd look at my torn-up dress, filthy from playing in the garden, and they'd say, 'Millie, you may have a terrible life now, but you save up your quarters and you'll be somebody someday.' Thing is, I never knew I wasn't somebody already, not until they told me that someday-part. I never thought my life was terrible."

We turned around and walked back up toward the house. "That was when I started noticing we were the poor folk living on the lake, and I resented my parents for it, until I realized, 'Who the hell are these rich ladies to tell me I have a terrible life?' I may be different, but maybe being different isn't a bad thing." She winked at me, like she thought I would know what being different was like. "And there are still a few of us odd birds from yesteryear hiding out on this million-dollar lake," she said in a way that made me wonder what she meant by *odd birds.*

She pointed to her small green two-story that seemed to shift to one side a little. "I could sell this lot for a fortune, easy. Had another offer this last year," she said, squeezing my arm as we walked back up the steps toward the house. "But it's my family home, and I'm gonna pass it down to my son, Benny, when Horace and I go, so he can have the stories and the memories inside it, so my great grandchildren can join the water skiing team like their great grand-mom did. So they can know how good it feels to be different on this lake."

I smiled to myself, picturing this little old lady on water skis.

"But now I want you to make me a promise, just like you promised your friend Bessilyn Hind."

I gasped. *How'd she know I was top-shelf crazy?*

"If Benny tries to sell this property after I go, you have a seance with him in this lake house. Tell him how his mom feels about it."

I smiled. "I promise. But I can't promise he'll listen."

She patted my hand with hers and brought me into the house. "You let me worry about that," she said.

It was warm in the living room and it smelled a lot like hard-boiled eggs and tuna. Her husband, a thin man with a hunch in his back, chopped an onion on the cutting board in the dining room. "Real nice of you to take those books," he said, hand shaking a little as he motioned with his knife.

"Horace is thrilled to have the garage back; can you tell?" Mildred said. "I suppose my grandson will be too. Instead of boarding up the lake house until next summer, we'll be letting him and his kids stay here."

She pointed toward the living room, and I finally noticed a bald man around 60 laying across her flowered couch, taking a nap. "My son, Benny. I'll wake him in a minute so he can help you out with those books. You wanna stay for dinner? Horace is making his specialty."

"Tuna casserole," he said. "The secret's eggs and butter."

"No thanks," I said, trying to make sure my face didn't look disgusted while I politely shook my head *no*. Tuna casserole with eggs *and butter* did not at all sound appealing, but I also had a sheriff to confront with a box full of evidence. And I still wasn't 100 percent sure I was right about Bessie's murder. I needed not only a plan, but a back-up one.

I heard the front door open and a little girl around five with curly dark hair and a chocolate-faced grin skidded into the room on her socks. She gave Mildred a hug.

"My little namesake," Mildred said. "Meet Lil Mil, that's what we call her." She gave the girl an extra squeeze. "Where are your shoes?"

"In the car."

I knelt down so I was eye level with the girl. "I'm Carly," I said, feeling that baby-obsession thing all over again. "I hear you get to stay on the lake this winter. Should be fun."

A man's voice called from the foyer. "Lil Mil, we've talked about this. You've gotta bring in your own shoes if you take 'em off in the car." I looked up and bit my lip. A tall man in his 30s with green eyes and light brown tousled hair came into the living room carrying a sparkly pink pair of buckle shoes in one hand and a three-year-old boy in the other. He saw me and quickly put the shoes on the counter to introduce himself. "I'm Mildred's grandson, Parker," he said with the kind of sparkle in his eyes that made me want to rethink dinner. Tuna casserole with eggs suddenly sounded amazing. Anything with eggs...

Why was I always thinking about eggs?

"This is Carly," Mildred said after I didn't remember to introduce myself. She took the boy, who even at about three years old almost rivaled his great grandmother's height. "Here, let me hold Benjamin while you help Carly load up her car with my books so I don't have to wake your dad."

"Take 'em all," Horace cackled a little too wildly for a shaky man with a knife. "Every dang box."

"He's been very supportive of my writing career over the years; can you tell?" Mildred laughed, throwing her husband a look.

"Come on," I said to Parker. "I'm the Civic out front." I turned to leave, but Mildred gently grabbed my arm. "Parker just got divorced," she whispered, not very quietly. Parker shook his head, and I smiled at him as we walked out to the garage.

"I apologize for my grandmother. She's always trying to set me up."

"Sounds like my mother," I said. "Only mine went so far as to make a profile for me on a dating site. One where I sound terribly desperate and I did not ask her to make it in the first place."

It was cold in the garage and it smelled like oil. Parker flicked on the light, and I let out a small gasp when I saw the stacks of boxes labeled *Mildred's Books.*

"I don't think they'll fit," I said, doing a quick mental count. I went to the back and lifted one of the boxes, quickly putting it back down again. I'd need help carrying them into my house too, and I only had a ghost and a possibly elderly dog to help me.

I took a couple boxes then told Parker I'd come back for the rest later that week.

"I should be here," he said. "But let me give you my number so you can text me to make sure."

I fumbled with my phone, almost dropping it when I pulled it out of my jacket pocket, momentarily forgetting how to create a new contact. I was too busy thinking about the cute outfit I was going to wear when I came back for the books and the witty things I would say to his kids.

After he went back inside, I sat in my car and looked at the photos on my phone before pulling out of Mildred's driveway, kicking myself for acting even more desperate than the dating profile my mother had made for me. But night-time strolls by the lake with a basket full of wine and cheese seemed anything but cliche right now.

I scrolled on, looking at the pictures I'd taken yesterday at the bed and breakfast before the channeling with Martha, the ones I took for my book.

I knew now the stains on the glove weren't grease and I needed to match the pattern on the fingertips to the pattern on the dress in order to prove it was used in the shooting. I looked around. I was still sitting in Mildred's long gravel driveway. Not the best place to reenact a murder. But I didn't see anyone peeking out at me from her neighbors' lake-mansions.

The evidence box was sitting on the passenger's seat, and I pulled out the gun and the glove.

It was strange to hold a weapon of any kind. Colder than I thought it'd be, lighter. I'm not sure why I expected warmth and heaviness.

The glove was also different in person than I thought it'd be, heavier, scratchier, and a lot droopier.

It was hard to hold the gun with what felt like a saggy oven mitt. But I was able to curl my finger around the trigger, remembering at the last second that there could still be a bullet in there. It was a remote possibility, but I didn't trust the police in Landover to empty a gun before selling it. And it would be just my luck to accidentally kill myself with a stray bullet from a 110-year-old piece of evidence.

The glove bunched up and flopped forward when I pointed the gun down at the angle it would have to have been angled at that night.

I brought up the photo on my phone of Bessilyn's dress and compared it with the glove. Back and forth. The patterns were similar, especially if the glove was bunched forward like it would have been if the hand in it had been smaller, like mine.

I glanced over at the police report, noticing for the first time that it had been signed by the police chief, Herbert Smalls. And in it, he talked about how he had apparently been at Bessilyn's party that night, and witnessed how upset Bessilyn had been.

I put the paper down. Herbert Smalls was the anti-suffragist guy. Doris Smalls's husband. No wonder the police were quick to write this case off as a suicide. The jerk probably didn't want to have to investigate a death he didn't see as worthy.

And suddenly I knew why the police had ignored blatant contradictory evidence. The glove with blood splatter should have been enough right there.

At least it was still enough to reopen the case. I took off the glove, something scraped along my thumb, and I turned the glove inside out to inspect it. A small green gem was embedded in the inside threads.

CHAPTER 24

BACK-UP PLANS

*J*t was evening when I got there. The sun was already setting. I took a deep breath and grabbed the box of evidence from my car.

I pretty much knew what Caleb's reaction was going to be when I showed him this proof, but I swore to a ghost I would do this, and I was going to keep my word. Plus, I had to return Paula's display items by 9:00 tonight or she was keeping my deposit. I didn't have time to think of a back-up plan.

The police station was on the corner of Main and Washington, just a little brick building with a flag out front and the words "City of Potter Grove Police Department" painted on the front window in block letters.

Justin leaned against a desk in the back next to Christine, a woman around 50 who was Shelby's biggest makeup customer.

I tried to seem as confident as I could, like what I was about to say was not at all crazy. I set my evidence box on the counter and waited for them to acknowledge me. "I need to see the sheriff. I'd like the police department to reopen a case."

"What's the case?" Justin asked, walking over to the counter, giving me a skeptical smile. "And what's in the box?"

"Evidence."

He nodded slowly. "Is this about Jackson? I know you think Destiny and Brock killed him, but there's not a lot we can do without getting the body exhumed..."

"They did kill him," I shot back. "But that's not what this is about."

Christine had short auburn hair and a thick coat of lipstick to match. "I think I know what this is about. The women's club has been talking about nothing else all month. The 100-year-old suffragette case. Most the vacationers are still around for this reason alone. My mother-in-law says she's never had more fun."

Justin peered over the box. "A hundred years? You serious?"

I looked him straight in the eye. "Yes. I'd like to know how to reopen a case that's more than 100 years old," I said. "One that's not considered a case yet."

Justin laughed then stopped when I didn't laugh with him. "Let me get Caleb," he finally said as he meandered down the hall, an almost saunter to his walk. At well over six feet, Justin's head almost grazed the door frame to the back. I thought I heard him add, "Just as stubborn as always."

I could hear Caleb before I saw him. His voice echoed off the walls of the small police lobby. "What? This is some kind of sick joke... Tell that woman I don't have time for her!"

"That woman can hear you," I yelled back. "And I'm not leaving until you make time."

Caleb's neck bones seemed to lead the way, protruding out at sharp, angry angles as he strutted to the front. I lifted the flap on the cardboard box and took a deep breath, prepared to make my statement. Christine practically ran to the counter to see what I was about to pull out.

"Bessilyn Margaret Hind did not kill herself in 1906."

"Is this what you do with your time now?" Caleb asked. "Think of ways to annoy hardworking folk?"

I ignored him. "And I have proof." I pulled out the police

report, the evidence tags, the gun, and the driving glove. Everything Paula allowed me to take from her display cases that morning. "These are all items Paula Henkel recently bought from this police department, correct?" I said.

Caleb rolled his eyes. "Old evidence taking up room that wasn't even part of an investigation. She can have it."

I nodded, pointing at the paper. "I think these were put in the evidence archives because somebody, even then, suspected something. And they were right. This glove alone proves Bessie Hind could not have committed suicide. On its evidence tag from 1906, it's described as being found outside, RS of house. Right side of house. And you can see it has a gunpowder pattern that matches the one on Bessie's dress." I pulled out my phone and brought the photo up of the champagne-colored gown on the mannequin in the display case.

I zoomed in on the spot. "I'm betting that's not grease on the fingertips, not when the dress has a similar pattern, proving the glove was there at the time of the shooting. And if this glove was found on the side of the house then there was no way the deceased could have taken it off and run it down there."

"Oh, I see why they love you at the country club. You're good," Christine said, clapping her hands a little.

"There's more," I said. I pulled the glove inside out and took the green gem out from the threads inside it. "This was stuck inside the glove. I'm not sure what it means, but I bet…"

Caleb laughed, interrupting me. "You know what I bet? I bet you think you're something else. Better than the police officers who already worked this case, huh? I saw that wire the other night at the seance. You're lucky I didn't say anything."

I tried to interrupt, but he waved a finger at me. "It's time you heard this. I don't like your kind. Good people don't start trouble. They wax their cars on Sundays. They bake casseroles and cookies for funeral wakes. Well, the women do." He looked at Justin and Christine for confirmation. They didn't nod. "Good people are busy. They don't raise the dead. They don't have time for hundred-year-old nonsense. Nobody cares about this anymore. It just makes more work."

Somehow, I resisted the urge to cuss the man out. "Regardless of how you feel about me, you have to open this case up again. The evidence proves it could not have been a suicide. Let me tell you about the window, and how the glove fit…"

"I don't have to do anything. And I don't care if all the ladies in Landover County got together and signed a little note saying, 'Pretty please, Sheriff Bowman, won't you reopen this case? You're so handsome and sweet…'"

I pointed my finger at him. "If you think, for one second, that's the way the Landover Ladies operate, you are more delusional than anyone gave you credit for, and we gave you credit for a lot of delusion."

He didn't even blink, so I went on. "I'm going to write a letter, all right, but not to you. To the Landover Gazette. I've got an interesting story about Bessilyn Hind's suicide I'm sure they will love to run. And the police officer standing in the way of her justice because he thinks I should be baking cookies for a wake."

"Ooooh, you should mention the Landover Ladies and the seance you did with them," Christine said, leaning over my evidence, apparently impressed. "Bessilyn Hind was one of the founding members, you know?"

"I should've known this was all a part of the show. You're still playing to your audience." Caleb burst out laughing. "The Landover Ladies really need to find better stuff to do with their time. Be sure to tell your mother-in-law I said that, Christine." He flicked the tiny green gem across the room.

Christine glared at him.

CHAPTER 25

BEAR NECESSITIES

I slammed my car door shut and yanked the evidence box from the passenger's seat. Things could not have gone worse for me. Rosalie was still mad I traded our seance money for a box of "damn evidence" to prove Bessie's case, and that box had pretty much meant nothing. Nothing. Caleb wouldn't even listen to me. I had more than a thousand books to pick up from Mildred's. I hadn't seen Bessie since the seance, and I had to return this box of evidence by the end of the night to Paula like I promised. Or she was charging me double.

At least I'd taken pictures of everything during my car reenactment. Maybe somebody would listen to me someday.

I threw open the door to the lobby, and looked around. It was darker than normal, and no one was there. The lobby was done in a dark Halloween theme, pumpkins and cornucopias strategically placed on tables and such, making the blood red wallpaper seem, well, bloodier.

The display cases had decorative museum lights now. Sir Walter's hat stared back at me. "I'm sorry I thought you killed her," I whispered to the ghost I knew was here somewhere.

I went over to the front desk and rang the bell. "Hello," I called into the creepy darkness. It was not like Paula to leave the place unattended. I helped myself to one of the cookies in the plastic cookie bin then swept the crumbs onto the floor. I rang the bell on the desk again and again. I finally texted her. "Where are you? I'm at your b&b. About to leave this box of evidence on the counter."

The room behind the desk had a light on, so I craned my neck to see if anyone was in there. A large shadow flickered around. I tiptoed over behind the desk, slowly approaching the room. That's when I heard it. Growling. I turned around and bolted, straight into the front desk computer, dropping my phone and almost falling.

"Rosalie wasn't crazy," I said to myself, noticing how large the shadow in the back room looked. "And now, whatever trashed her store is in there." I wasn't sure if it was a shapeshifting bear or a skull-crushing bird. I almost yelled out Bobby's name when a horrible thought came to me. *What if Paula was already killed by whatever was in there?*

I looked around for a weapon, deciding on the large metal Halloween candlestick on the front counter for decoration. Whatever animal was in the back room was still growling, almost huffing, in low gravelly tones that made me think it was pretty large. I went around the customer side of the front desk area again, holding the candlestick up over my head, but mostly looking for my phone so I could call 911. I didn't seriously think the candlestick was going to do much good despite its street cred in the game of Clue.

I kept my distance, staying far enough away that I had time to run. Good thing I knew the old Hind House pretty well by now. There was a garden room off the back I could escape to. And I inched toward it, looking at the office as I passed it, fully expecting to see it trashed with blood, guts, and gore. Instead I smelled fish.

What the?

A large white furry head looked up at me from behind the desk of Paula's cushy office suite. Its mouth was in a metal bucket, but when it saw me, it stopped chomping and stood up. A huge, thick polar bear.

I held in my scream and quickly backed my way down the hall toward the garden room.

It padded slowly around the desk, knocking over the decorative globe behind it. It stopped and roared, mouth open extra wide, like it was trying to tell me to stop walking away already and just succumb to being part of the snack.

"Nice bear. Go back to your fish," I said. As soon as I'd backed up out of its sight, I took off down the hall toward the patio room. The beast was right behind me. I could hear its heavy paws thumping and skidding along the floorboards. I closed the garden room door and took a deep breath, my heart still racing. In my wildest dreams on possible ways to die, polar bear attack was pretty far down the list.

I flicked on the light, and looked around for a phone, wondering if I should run out the back door or stay put. I didn't hear polar bear breath along the doorway like I thought I would. Maybe it went back to its fish. Or maybe I'd imagined the whole thing. Maybe I'd been hallucinating again.

Hallucinations were sure making my life confusing.

The garden room was spacious with huge glass windows for walls, a wicker chair patio set was next to a wrought iron one. Bookcases on every wall were filled with tacky vases, along with old framed black-and-white photos of the early 1900s.

This was the room where Henry Bowman, his wife, and the other "wealthy outcasts" had hidden themselves away so they wouldn't have to keep their conversations polite that night.

A large photo of a garden party with women in white dresses and parasols hung on the back wall, reminding me how condescending and awful they'd been to Bessie on her birthday.

I shook my head at the painting. Even at a garden party, the dresses were huge and intricate... except for Eliza's and Pleasant's.

"A simple frock, perfect for slipping into pant legs," I said. "Pleasant..."

The picture crashed to the floor, shattering on the tile. And the lights went out.

"Show yourself now," I yelled with as much authority as I could muster. No one materialized. I blinked into the darkness, trying to get my eyes to adjust to the moonlight. A vase shot across the room at me, almost hitting me on the hand.

"Pleasant, I know it was you."

The hazy glowing outline of an older woman dressed all in black appeared in the shadows. She looked very different than she had at the party, her face sunken and hollow, more like the way Mrs. Nebitt described her.

"I've been riding on you for a while, following you," she said.

"And you didn't say 'hi' to your sister?"

Another vase shot across the room. This one hit me square in the shoulder. Pain shot down my back. I should've known better than to get mouthy with a ghost.

She was coming at me now. Books and knickknacks seemed to fly from her fingertips as she moved. I ducked behind a chair, covering my head with one of its cushions.

"You couldn't leave well enough alone," she said. She was a very powerful ghost. I could tell, even more powerful than Bessilyn, and Bessie had Jackson beat by a mile.

"It's over, Pleasant. We've figured it out, and nothing is going to change about that, no matter how many knickknacks and vases you hit me with. But don't you want to end this burden once and for all? This secret you've been lugging around?"

I was really putting my ad-lib skills to the test here. Having to negotiate with an antique-throwing ghost was as surprising to me tonight as being mauled by polar bear.

She didn't stop. She rushed at me, passing through the chair I was hiding behind, chilling every one of my bones instantly.

Her attention went to the back of the room.

"You have a lot of nerve," said a loud booming voice that seemed to echo off the wall behind me. The large picturesque windows that showcased the backyard blew out in the patio room, one after the other, shattering glass onto the courtyard and garden. I knew who it was before she even showed herself. But then, there was really only one ghost I knew who made glass-breaking her MO.

Bessilyn appeared right in front of her sister. She was very bright and very large compared to Pleasant. "You! Killed! Me!"

I knew from Jackson that most ghosts repelled each other if they got too close. Bessie seemed to use that energy to her advantage. She rushed at her sister, knocking Pleasant across the room.

I curled tighter under my chair, unsure what damage a sister-ghost fight was going to do, but totally sure I was going to be asked to pay for it.

Pleasant got up and made herself larger too. "I've always hated you," she screamed, throwing a vase at her sister. It went right through Bessilyn, crashing along the tile of the garden room. "You were never the same after I had the kids. You didn't care anymore!" Pleasant tossed a chair at her this time.

Bessie caught it mid-air and set it down. "Stop, Pleasant. It was Troy. That's why I never came over. After you had the kids, all you wanted from me was for me to be your nanny. That's all you wanted from any of us. Mom, Dad, Popsy…"

"No. And you know it." Pleasant's color faded and she grew smaller again. "I only wanted you to be my sister. I needed help with those kids and my marriage. I needed advice. I didn't know what I was doing. Mom was no help. I needed a sister. And you only cared about your stupid clubs and causes." They were both quiet now, hovering close but not touching. "You were jealous of me and my family. Admit it."

Bessie's face turned white. "If I was, it was only because Mother talked a lot about your children... her precious grand-children... Yes, you were the one who did everything right and perfect, and I shouldn't have been jealous that you were rewarded for it, but you're right, I was."

This seemed to calm Pleasant down. Her voice was weaker when she spoke. "It was Troy's idea," Pleasant said. "He always said things like, 'Why does Bessie get all the money? We deserve better. Our children will never have the proper upbringing they deserve with nannies and a large house because Bessie will always be a financial burden on your parents. She's never going to leave.' I let him convince me you were doing it on purpose, draining all our parents' money, refusing to leave and get married."

I peeked out from my hiding spot behind the metal chair. Pleasant's ghostly white face showed years of regret, hanging off of her in unpleasant sags.

She went on, looking down at her dress as she talked. "He picked the fight on purpose. It was completely planned so you'd go upstairs and sulk into your sleeping pills. If anyone noticed me following, they wouldn't think much of a woman consoling her sister, but no one saw me. The whole time I went up those stairs, I kept wishing someone would notice..."

"I bet," Bessilyn said. "What did you use? Father's chloroform?"

Pleasant nodded. "It only took a little splash and you were out like a light, just like Troy said would happen. He put everything in place. Father's trousers and jacket under your bed, so I could stuff my dress inside the pant legs. Troy said I needed to do that so if I got caught, it would look like a man had done it, and of course, he would have an alibi. He made it sound so natural, like something you should already be doing, killing yourself at this point in your life because you were 35 and useless."

"Useless?" Bessie said.

"He killed our parents too," Pleasant replied.

"I knew it," I yelled. "The car accident." Both ghosts looked at me like they couldn't believe I was trying to join their conversation, and I sank back behind my chair again.

Pleasant's voice was even louder now. "Six months after you passed away, so did our parents. Troy cut their brakes. He never admitted it, and I never asked. But I saw him looking under the hood of Father's car just before they went out on their country drive to the mountains to try to take their minds off your death." She tugged on the long sleeve of her stiff-looking dress. "I never forgave myself. I became a bitter, angry woman."

I crawled out again. "And after their death, that's when it came out that your family had nothing. No money. Just debt." They both glared at me. I went back behind the chair.

"I don't believe it," Bessie said.

Pleasant went on. "It's true. We had to sell the house, the cannery too. For pennies." She hovered across the room, staring out at the night. "I'm sorry," she said to Bessie. "I know sorry doesn't mean much now..."

Bessie faded and so did her sister just as the lights came back on. The room was quiet, calm. Pieces of vase and window were all over the floor and the table. Chairs were overturned and the large photo frame that contained the garden party scene was broken into bits. Cold air swirled all around the room from the broken windows.

But I was okay. I took a deep breath and shook out my limbs until it suddenly occurred to me I still had a possible polar bear problem to deal with.

I listened at the door, but didn't hear anything. No growling. No roaring. Nothing but a knock.

"Hello?" I said.

"Hello," Paula said back. "Carly Mae? I was just texting you.

When you said you were at the bed and breakfast, I didn't know that meant you were hiding in my garden room. I saw my evidence box on the counter, and I found your phone. I've also got my checkbook. I'm ready to pay you for the seance and be done with this."

I reluctantly opened the door. She shoved my phone at me then turned toward the mess.

Her face grew bright red. "You are paying for this," she screamed over and over. "I should call the police."

I looked down at my phone. My screen was cracked, of course. But it was working. I ignored her tantrum and checked it over thoroughly.

She continued yelling. "And to think, I was just about to pay you. You're not getting anything now. Anything. You hear me? Not even a quarter. You probably owe me money. What in the hell happened here?"

I looked up at her. Her nostrils were flaring, eyes bugging.

I pulled a chunk of fish out of her hair. "Polar bear," I said. "That's what happened." I flicked the fish onto the floor next to some glass.

Paula opened her mouth like she was going to say something, but stopped.

"Yep, a polar bear," I said. I turned my phone toward her, showing her the photo I'd accidentally taken when I dropped my phone earlier. The screen was cracked but you could still see the white fur and fangs of an animal (one with a lot of human features), behind the half-closed door of her office. "Police ought to be on the lookout for that. Don't you think? I bet it's what tore up Rosalie's shop and scared Delilah Scott... Maybe, it broke the windows at the seance too. That would be a lot more believable than a ghost, seeing how I have a photo of this very real bear. And ghosts are malarkey."

She licked her pen and held out her checkbook. "What do I owe you again?"

"Half the gross price. The exact number we worked out before," I said as she wrote. "And we're calling it even on damages. I charge a fee for deleting my polar bear photos."

I snatched the check and walked out.

CHAPTER 26

SEEING REASON

*L*ooking like she just came off the lake in her crisp red boat shoes, matching shorts, and striped cardigan, Amelia strutted up to the front door of the police department with me and about 15 of her country club friends.

"Where'd you say you were from again?" she asked me, her dyed-brown bob swinging naturally with her stride.

"Indianapolis," I answered.

"I'm originally from Indiana too, Lake Tippecanoe. Here's what these turkeys don't know about us Hoosiers," she winked at me. "We kick butt the same way we grow corn. In mile-long, ain't-we-done-with-this-yet stretches of it."

I smiled. I was really starting to like this woman. Her daughter-in-law, Christine, was behind the computer when we all stormed into the lobby. She hurried into the back as soon as she saw us. "Sheriff! You've got some visitors." She sounded like a kid announcing Christmas.

Caleb strutted out, wiping his fingers on a napkin, the smell of chicken wafting up from the back room. His face fell when he saw all the ladies taking up the whole entryway of the small police station's lobby. "I... uh... what's all this about, Christine?"

"Sorry to interrupt your dinner, Sheriff Bowman," Christine's mother-in-law said. "I'm Amelia Mayfair. You obviously know my daughter-in-law."

He gave Christine a look as if to ask, "Just what in the hell is going on here? And why wasn't I properly warned?"

Christine only smiled, lipstick on her teeth the whole time.

Amelia continued. "You may also know this woman here." She put her arm around me, squeezing me tighter than I thought a bony woman could squeeze. "One of the finest mediums I've ever met. I tell you. I'll believe anything she says. And so should you. That's why you're gonna open Ms. Bessilyn Hind's case back up and turn it from a suicide to a murder..."

"The hell I will," Caleb said. "You all are crazy. I don't even know if it's possible to do that, but I am certainly not going to find out. That thing's more than a hundred years old, and nobody cares."

"I thought you might say that." She placed her cell phone on the counter. "Go ahead, Mayor Bowman," she said. "Your turn."

Caleb looked at the phone like it might bite his hand off. "Uh... Dad?"

The voice was stern and gravelly. "Caleb, yes, it's your father. I'm going to make this brief because I cannot for the life of me know why I even have to make such a foolhardy phone call. Do what these ladies want. They came to you in earnest with evidence that contradicts the work of your fellow police officers. It doesn't matter if it happened now or 300 years ago. You take that evidence and you do what's right. Everyone's lives matter, and so do their deaths. And as mayor of this town, it's my job to make sure we all know that."

Caleb didn't say anything. His face turned about three colors of red.

"Caleb, did you hear me?"

"Yes, I heard," he said. "I'll look into it."

"You'll do more than that. You'll handle it."

The mayor went on. "Ladies, I apologize that you had to come down here. We will handle all the details. You just go on home, being rest assured that those details will be handled. I saw the evidence myself, including the photo of Pleasant from the night of that party. She was wearing earrings that looked like the gem I saw in the pictures of that glove. Bessilyn Hind was murdered by her sister. Period. End of story."

He hung up.

Amelia scooped up her cell phone. "Thank you for your time. I'm glad you can finally see reason," she said, as we walked toward the door. She winked at me again as soon as we were outside. "More than half the country club contributes heavily to the mayor's campaign."

We took about a million victory pictures in front of the police station for the country club's wall before everyone hugged and shook hands. Most of the ladies were vacationers here, and I knew I wouldn't see them again until next summer. I slowly got into my car, already feeling the loneliness of a winter coming.

The whole way up Gate Hill, I thought I felt a presence beside me. I knew who it was, too. I turned toward the passenger's seat. "Did you see that, Bessie," I said to the ghost I now had a feeling had been traveling with me for a while. "Your case is officially closed."

She materialized in the seat beside me. "Please tell the ladies I am forever grateful for their help. Yours, as well."

"I'm sorry it was your sister."

"I am too," she said, staring out the window at the woods and dirt surrounding Gate Hill. "As it turns out, you don't stop learning about life after you die."

I threw my foot on the gas, easily maneuvering around the potholes and rocks that I had memorized along the dirt road up to my place. The sun was setting, but even in the shadows of dusk, I knew how to avoid the bumps by now.

I turned back toward my guest, unsure of how this all worked. "So, are you moving on?"

She tilted her head. "Wherever would I go?"

"Wherever ghosts go when their cases have been solved," I said, trying not to be too presumptuous.

"Doubtful," she replied. "I'm the star of the bed and breakfast, you know. I can't see me wanting to move on anytime soon. I like it where I'm at with Walter, Pleasant, and Martha. Plus, my case isn't done yet, which brings me to my next point of business…"

JUSTIN'S MUSCLES bulged through his t-shirt as he lifted another box out of the back of his truck a few days later. I shut the tailgate behind him then watched as he struggled to put it on the dolly. These boxes were heavy and there were a lot of them. "The last one," I said. "Thanks for helping me get Mildred's books."

It was oddly warm today, like summer wasn't quite done throttling us yet, even though it was technically fall now. Sweat soaked the back of his shirt, and I got a whiff of musky cologne as I caught up to him so I could open the kitchen door.

My ex-husband materialized on the veranda next to me as soon as the deputy stepped inside. "He's flexing on purpose," Jackson said, rolling his eyes. "You know that, right? It's so pathetic how petty the living can be."

"Almost as petty as the dead," I whispered back so low Justin wouldn't hear.

Rex growled from the kitchen when he saw Justin with the boxes. He didn't always growl at Justin, but it happened a lot.

'Rex, stop," I said, grabbing his collar. I stroked my golden lab's fur, trying to calm him down, but I could feel his back muscles tightening.

"I rest my case." Jackson motioned toward the shaking

labrador. "Even my dog knows a phony when he sees one, and there's something phony about Justin Fortworth."

He did have a point. Rex liked just about everyone, but for some odd reason, not always Justin, which made me not always trust Justin one-hundred percent.

"I don't know what's gotten into him," I said to the deputy, pulling Rex back. "I'll take him upstairs."

"Don't bother" Justin replied. "I have to head into work soon anyway."

We both looked at each other for a second, until I looked away. There were too many things between us for there to be room for anything else, I reminded myself. We tried this twelve years ago, and it ended awfully.

"I should go," he said.

"I'll walk you out," I let go of my lab who seemed to relax knowing Justin was leaving.

Justin stopped in the doorway and ran a nervous hand through his thick, moppy brown hair.

"For what it's worth," he said. "I didn't start those rumors about you being a gold digger way back when."

I studied his eyes, looking for any telltale signs he wasn't telling the truth, but only my mother had those. "It's okay. I was dumb and nineteen, and the rumors were more accurate than I like to admit. I didn't always make good choices."

"Looks like you're making better ones now," he said, motioning toward my wall of books just inside the living room. I laughed.

He leaned into me, his head tilted, his eyes on my lips, and my heart jumped into my throat.

Was he going to kiss me?

I pulled away. I wasn't ready for that, not yet. I still didn't trust this man.

He looked down at his boots, his face growing red under his tannish skin. "I should go."

I knew now what Bessilyn meant when she said Justin was my Walter. I was pretending not to care. I'd made one of my famous "I deserve better" speeches when I broke up with this man years ago right before I went out with Jackson. And I'd been wrong. But, I still couldn't admit that.

He turned back toward the door, and I watched him leave. Was my pride really going to let me lose him again, like Bessie lost Walter?

"Wait," I said, walking out to the veranda after him. He turned around. I stood on my tiptoes and kissed his cheek. It was scratchy and warm, and I wanted to pull him in closer, but I stopped. "Thanks for helping me with the..."

"You wanna get coffee sometime?" he asked, his arm on the dolly.

My ex appeared by my side. "Honestly," he said, motioning toward Justin. "He's flexing again. You see that, right? Who flexes while leaning casually? You know what they say about men who flex all the time. Overcompensating..."

"Please stop and go away. This is confusing enough," I said to him, realizing how that sounded to Justin, because no one could ever see the ghosts I talked to. "I... I wasn't talking to you, Justin."

He nodded.

I knew it needed more of an explanation. "I was talking to a ghost just then, actually. I'm sorry. I talk to ghosts. And now that you know I'm weird, I totally get it if you tell me you don't actually have time for coffee."

"You wanna get that coffee this Saturday?" he said, walking down the steps of the veranda. "Maybe dinner's less confusing. I can pick you up at six. We'll talk more about your ghost issues then."

"Perfect," I said, a little shocked. I didn't mention the part where the ghosts might ride along with us or that the main ghost was Jackson. It was probably best to take one crazy moment at a time.

Justin left and I almost wanted to call my mother. I was weird. I worked retail. And I had a date on Saturday with a wonderful man who knew those things about me and thought I was wonderful back. I didn't even need to lie about anything.

I sat on the couch and grabbed a stack of books, opening one up to the bed and breakfast's spot. I smoothed in the sticker I'd made for it, reading it to myself.

For more than 110 years, it was believed this founding member of the Women's Club in Landover, Wisconsin shot herself in the heart over a break-up with her fiancé, millionaire Sir Walter Timbre. But the case was reopened and declared a homicide, in large part because of the help from the Landover Country Club's Women's Club of today.

Bessie appeared. Her smile took over her entire face when she saw the books. "Splendid!" she said, reading the label over. "But you forgot the part where I most definitely do not walk the halls of the bed and breakfast calling out for 'Walty.' That simply does not happen. So, add that in there too." She motioned for me to get moving.

I glared at her. "You have got to be kidding me. I already printed the stickers out."

"I'm sure pens still work for retractions in the modern age."

I stomped over to the credenza on the far side of the room, searching for a pen so I could write in every single book that this dead women's-rights leader definitely did not spend her nights pining for a man while yelling out a cutesy nickname, even though we both knew she did do that.

I caught a glimpse of my cute boots as I walked, and smiled to myself. I used to think nothing good was ever in my section, like "good" was something life bestowed on some while denying to others. And that I would always have to settle.

My life was good now. Maybe it always had been, but I could see it clearly now. Not just in spite of my dead ex-husband, but because of him. And that's what scared me the most. I was getting swept up in this curse. And I didn't want any of it to end.

Rex brushed against my leg just as I spotted the newspaper article I printed out about the hero dog and the birds. I pulled it out from the drawer and looked from the grainy black-and-white photo of the dog in 1954 to my own dog. *What on earth made me think my dog could possibly be this one?*

My eyesight flickered and the room suddenly went black. I realized I was clutching the dining room table, but only because I felt its smooth wood under my fingernails. I couldn't actually see a thing. My heart raced as I fumbled and grasped for a dining room chair, trying to understand just what in the hell was going on. I managed to sit down as something brushed against my leg that felt very much like a large feathered fan. The sound of flapping wings filled the room, thick and monstrous.

"Rex," I called, my voice frantic. "Jackson."

Through flickering spots of light, I saw a dark shadow by my leg that I momentarily thought to be an enormous bird.

My ex materialized beside me, and I could see him perfectly. "Are you okay?" he asked.

Hallucinations. Flickering eyesight. These were all signs Rosalie had warned me about.

I looked down at my leg. Rex stepped out from under the table, away from the shadows and into the light of the room. Just a normal-sized dog, not a gigantic bird brushing along my pant leg.

"I'm fine," I said to my ex after a second. "It's nothing."

Neither one of us believed me.

The End

≈

READ on to the next chapter for a sneak peek of book three called *Behind the Boater's Cover-up.*

If you'd like to get the Christmas novella in this series free, just sign up for my list at ettafaire.com. You'll also be the first to know when new books are coming out.

And please, if you have the time, I would really appreciate it if you could review this book. Indie authors, like me, need every review we can get. Thanks!

Find a typo or other editing error? Please, email me at etta@ettafaire.com and let me know, and I'll fix it right away. I try my best to put out the best product possible, but I'm far from perfect, so I appreciate your help and support on that.

From the back cover:

When paranormal becomes your new normal,
The only thing certain in life
Is that it will involve death.

Locals refer to it as Accident Loop, the part of Landover Lake where "the accident" happened in 1957.

According to legend, a group of high-school graduates went late-night partying on a boat after the country club's sock hop ended early, but they didn't return. Some say they drowned. Some say they got run over by a boat. But everyone agrees it was an accident. Until now.

Gloria Thomas, one of the partiers that night, wants Carly's help to figure out the truth about what happened, and she says it was no accident. Through channeling with the woman's ghost, Carly is taken straight to that night to relive the dance, the after party, the young woman's death, and the obvious cover-up.

But while channeling memories from the 1950s, Carly gets to know the younger versions of her older friends and the shocking way the boating "accident" was handled. Will she learn the hard way that stirring a pot from yesteryear can still leave you burned today?

Find out by reading *Behind the Boater's Cover-Up*, the third book in the paranormal mystery series, The Ghosts Of Landover Mysteries.

BEHIND THE BOATER'S COVER-UP

CHAPTER ONE: DATE KILLERS

I realized I was making my ice-skating face again. My cheeks naturally scrunched into an odd, fake smile whenever I had to pretend to adore something I really hated. It wasn't something I had control over, and it happened whether I was on the ice or not.

Snow fell along my path. My toes were numb in the skates I'd had since I was 14 and swore to my mother that my feet were done growing so she could go ahead and buy those expensive skates that everyone else had at school because *I just loved ice skating*. That day marked the beginning of my ice-skating face. I make that face a lot around my dead ex-husband now, whenever he wants to buddy up and solve another murder together.

The five-year-old little pink puff in front of me skated backwards, sticking out her tongue. "Come on, slow poke," Lil Mil said, wiggling her hips in a mocking fashion. I tried to catch up but I lost my balance and fell into the six-foot, dark-haired man skating by my side.

"Don't worry," Justin said. "She'll come 'round again in a second. You can catch her next time."

His already large arm was made even thicker by the puffer

jacket he was wearing. We'd been dating for three months now, and it was nice, but not serious. I wasn't sure if I was ready for serious yet, but I was sure enjoying the nice part.

Partiers' Loop was the one part of the lake everyone came to ice skate on whenever the weather permitted, and it was packed with people today, enjoying a winter Sunday on Landover Lake. Soft rock music played out from the speakers that someone had set up along the side. I tugged Justin in tighter, trying to warm myself on his chest as we passed under a tree limb.

I watched every branch intently as we went under, not quite trusting nature just yet, not after Delilah Scott said she heard "those birds" again last week.

Mrs. Carmichael came up behind me and grabbed my arm, making me lose my footing and fall onto the ice, mostly because I'd been thinking about the birds. Pain shot up my back, but I tried to laugh it off.

She put out a gloved hand to help me up. "Sorry about that, Carly Mae. You would think that's why they call this Accident Loop, wouldn't ya?" She looked different without her pink Spoony River uniform on. Her blonde hair was dotted with gray and flew crazily out of her knit cap as she talked. In or out of the diner, Mrs. Carmichael was still hands down the town's biggest gossip. And I could tell, she couldn't wait to tell me something here.

"I thought it was called Partier's Loop," I said.

"Same thing." Old George grunted by her side. He pointed down to the ice we were skating on. "Terrible boating accident happened on this side of the lake." His voice sounded straight out of a horror movie.

"Let me tell it," Mrs. Carmichael teased, hitting his arm in a way that made me wonder if old George and Mrs. Carmichael were becoming the town's latest bit of gossip. "Sometime in the 1950s. Oh no, it was the 1960s... Oh I don't know. A while back, some kids went partying on a boat after dark. Four people didn't come back. Drowned."

"No, they got run over by their boat, mangled in the propeller," George said.

"They drowned. They were high and drunk and they swam too far from the boat. Their bloated remains washed up right here." She pointed.

He shook his head and she shot him a look.

"Well, it's a lovely story either way," I said, making Justin smile at me as the older couple skated on still arguing over the gruesome details.

Justin was a man of few words, but I was really enjoying the quiet way he communicated, especially since I lived with a loud-mouthed ghost of an ex-husband.

We skated by Parker Blueberg, who was off to the side holding onto his three-year-old son's back as they shuffled slowly along the ice. The kid could barely move he was so bundled up, but he sported a wild grin and rosy chubby cheeks.

"Thanks for inviting us," Parker said when he saw me watching him. He had his hood down, and his thick sandy brown hair was flaked with snow. He smiled just enough to show he probably wore his retainer a lot more than I did; perfectly straight, white teeth.

Justin pulled me in tighter.

"Of course," I said as we skated over to him. "You're the newbies in town. And this is the best entertainment we have here in January. Cheapest too. Okay, it's the only entertainment. Sorry."

"I'm always looking for cheap entertainment for the kids," he said. "Mostly because I'm also still looking for a job."

I turned to Justin. "Parker was a personal trainer back in Chicago."

"No kidding." Justin puffed out his chest. "What do you bench?"

"I mostly taught spin class and yoga."

"That's bike riding, right? You taught bike riding to grown-ups."

"It's a little more complicated than that," Parker said.

"Two-fifty," Justin replied, still puffing out his chest, which made me wonder if he'd exhaled yet. "I bench two-fifty."

"If I hear of anything, I'll let you know," I said and skated ahead, leaving the testosterone competition behind.

Jackson appeared by my side. "Well, they certainly are impressive, aren't they." He motioned toward the men behind us. "You don't often see two jocks using almost complete sentences at the same time."

I hit a slippery patch and struggled to catch my footing again. "Go away," I muttered under my breath to the annoying ghost hovering by me. My ex-husband's coloring seemed particularly pale against the snow surrounding us, his full beard and thin frame fading into the background. I looked around before saying anything else, just to make sure no one was watching me. I tried to avoid looking crazy in public, whenever possible. And no one else could see the ghosts I talked to. "You promised you wouldn't go with me on dates. You're being a date killer again."

"I'm actually here on official business, not as a date killer. Although you seem to be your own biggest date killer right now."

I turned to him, hands on my hips.

"Come on, Carly doll," he said, raising an almost transparent eyebrow at me. "Why did you invite Parker and the kids along on a date with Justin?"

"I thought the kids would like this, and... I don't need to answer that. Justin and I are happy. What's your official business?"

"That boating accident they were talking about. One of the partiers is coming home with us."

"Of course he is. Let me guess. It wasn't an accident."

"It's a she. And no. She's absolutely certain it wasn't, but she doesn't remember what happened. She's been waiting a long time for a strong medium to come to this part of Landover Lake so she could finally figure things out. It's why she haunts here. Since 1957."

I nodded, but my face felt oddly frozen when I moved it. I was ready to head inside, defrost, and get some hot chocolate.

Jackson continued. "She's also got strong memories from 1954." His voice took a sing-songy lilt to it. He knew that was going to be the kicker. A ghost with memories from 1954 was too enticing for me to pass up. I'd recently started a keepsake box full of articles and information from 1954 and a little bit of 1955, the years when the strange growling crows with large yellowed beaks had taken over Potter Grove, apparently dive-bombing victims' skulls seemingly at random. They killed five people and seriously wounded several more before leaving the area as mysteriously as they came.

A few people believed they were back. I was one of them.

"You don't need to convince me," I said to my ex. "I was already going to do it."

Justin skated up and took my hand again. "You were already going to do what?" he asked, turning his head to the side. Justin knew I was a medium. He knew I talked to ghosts at my haunted house, and I could tell he was slowly starting to believe that maybe they weren't just pretend friends. But I never told him they sometimes followed me around or that I more than occasionally helped them solve a murder case or two. I needed to ease people into my crazy.

"Nothing," I said, pulling my hat off so I could adjust it over my blondish-brown curls in a way that would hopefully frame my face in something that looked cute and not clownish. "You ready to go?"

The wind picked up, blowing my hat off my fingers and sending it sliding along the ice. Of course this also made my hair fly out in all directions, and I struggled to press it back down to normal-poof as I skated after my hat. My nose dripped and my ears stung, and I realized after a while that I was skating with my tongue out, but I'd paid way too much for that cute hat to let it go that easily. It landed under the tree limb, and I bent down to grab it. Parker did too, and our hands touched. Technically, our gloves.

"Sorry," I said, pulling my hand back like he'd assaulted me.

Parker smiled and handed me my hat. "Thanks again. We had a great time."

"You too." I said. "I mean, me too. I had a great time too."

"Oh my. Awkward," my ex-husband said, popping in to commentate. I ignored the annoying ghost. "Don't mind me," Jackson continued. "I only wonder if your boyfriend is watching this completely natural exchange with the man you invited on your date."

As soon as Parker left, I glared at Jackson. "There is nothing wrong here. I only invited this man to this lake because I told Mildred I would help her grandson acclimate to the area." I tried to remember if I actually said that to Mildred or not.

"Tell yourself whatever you want," Jackson replied.

The wind pummeled my face again but this time I heard a low, humming kind of a noise along with it. It lifted along the breeze, an almost growling sound. Like nothing I'd ever heard before, different than the growls at the bed and breakfast months ago. It was almost human sounding.

I looked all around, searching the branches overhead for the birds I knew must be there, a chill running up my spine. When the wind died down, I covered my skull and shushed my ex-husband even though he wasn't talking and listened intently to the wind again. But I didn't hear anything else.

It had to have been my imagination. I was just being paranoid. Still, I quickly caught up to Justin who was sitting on the bench, putting his boots on, oblivious to the hat hunt and the birds growling. I scooted in close and grabbed his hand faster than I'd intended.

"Let's go," I said.

"That's what we're doing, right?" He shrugged. "You gonna change out of your skates?"

"Nope," I replied, not even listening to my mother's nagging voice echoing through my head about how she knew I wasn't going to take care of those expensive skates. I stood up and wobbled across the snow and dirt in them.

Justin didn't say much as we trudged over to his truck while we held hands, me trying to make the pace as fast as possible in a clunky pair of ice skates as I checked all the branches along the way. When we reached the parking lot, he looked back at the makeshift skating rink set up along the ice behind us, his eyes wet from the wind. "Spin class and yoga," he said, shaking his head.

I looked back too just in time to see a very large crow flying across the rink toward the bench where Justin and I had just been sitting. I couldn't move. I just stood, holding onto the truck door, staring at the tree. The bird looked completely normal, yet something seemed off.

"You okay?" Justin asked, starting the truck, motioning for me to get in.

Squinting into the wind, I caught the eye of another black bird. This one was in a higher branch when our eyes met. A bigger one. It seemed to be looking for me too, with a surprisingly human glare, and a thick yellowed beak.

BEHIND THE BOATER'S COVER-UP

CHAPTER TWO: ACCIDENTS HAPPEN, SOMETIMES ON PURPOSE

J snuggled into the crook of Justin's arm and tried to focus on the superhero movie streaming on my flatscreen. Justin smelled like soap mixed with sex appeal, and he was wearing the dark gray sweater I told him I couldn't resist. But still, the only thing I could think about was my ex-husband and the partier we'd just taken home with us.

They were here somewhere, watching and waiting, probably tapping on their ghost watches.

Rex sat quietly at our feet. My dog was finally getting used to my boyfriend. He used to bark at Justin a lot, but it only happened every once in a while now.

"Did I tell you," Justin said, leaning over toward me. "You look beautiful tonight?"

"It's completely okay if you repeat yourself. I hear that's a sign of extreme intelligence."

He brushed a strand of my curls away from my face and moved in for a kiss. His face was wonderfully scratchy and soft all at the same time. He ran a hand along the back of my neck as he pressed his lips over mine and a tingle ran all the way to my toes. I was just starting to get into it when I opened my eyes for a split second. Jackson was hovering directly above us.

I closed my eyes again and tried to ignore him. *He's just looking for attention, and if you give it to him, things will only continue down this path,* I told myself like I was dealing with a toddler and not a 50-something-year-old ghost.

I peeked again. He was still there. The man was bound and determined to break Justin and me up, again. Twelve years ago, I broke up with Justin to date and marry Jackson, and it wasn't about to happen again, not that you could date and marry a dead guy. Or that I would want to.

Justin stopped kissing me and pulled away. "Is something wrong?' he asked.

"No. It's nothing," I replied, mostly for the benefit of the hovering ghost.

"It's your ex again, huh?" he said. He looked around my living room. "I think I like hanging out at my place better. No offense."

"None taken. I'm sorry."

"It's okay," he said in a way that made me think it really wasn't. "I have to get up early anyway."

It was a sore spot all the way around. Even though Justin would never admit it, I knew he resented Jackson again, and probably wondered if I was even making him up.

I followed my boyfriend to the kitchen where he paused at the back door that led to the veranda. "Next time, my place," he said, gently lifting my chin up with the tip of his finger so he could kiss me again. Then he left. And my heart sunk into my gut.

These ghosts were ruining my love life.

Plus, I didn't really want to hang out at Justin's apartment all the time. That place gave me the creeps, and this was from a woman who lived in a haunted house. His apartment complex sat right at the edge of the Dead Forest, a wildlife preserve that spanned a whole side of Landover County, reaching for miles, like a divider that kept us apart from the rest of civilization. Every place in Landover had its myths. You couldn't live here and not know about them. But the Dead Forest had the creepiest one. People who went into the Dead Forest didn't come out, hence the name. And it was this fact that made the myth so creepy. Nobody knew why people didn't return because nobody returned.

Logically, I knew it was just a rumor. And, I'd never actually heard of anyone going into the forest. But when you live in a town where rumors seem to be proving themselves true right and left, you don't test things. You don't decide to be that person who goes in.

So now, because my jerk of an ex-husband was ruining my love life, my only choices were be the pervy ghost's sex show or hang out by death's forest.

Of course Jackson appeared as soon as the door closed. "I thought he'd never leave," he said.

"He shouldn't have to. He's my boyfriend."

"Just until someone better wins you back." He winked.

"So your plan is to annoy your way back into my heart?"

"Worked the first time."

I grabbed one of the dishes drying along the side of the sink and somehow resisted the urge to chuck it out the window. I needed privacy around here. I needed to be free from this house agreement and these ghosts. Clutching the dish so hard I almost broke it with my bare hands, I gently placed it into the cabinet where it belonged. One after another. Then, I grabbed Rex's dog food and plopped it into the microwave. The thermometer to check the food's temperature was right where it always was. Everything was always right where it should be. Things were too routine. Too strict.

"No wonder I'm 31 and still dating. Justin's not going to stick around if he has to put up with weird house rules and ex-husband ghosts."

"Now, Carly. If a boy really likes you for you," Jackson began. "He won't care."

"Oh shut up," I replied as the microwave beeped. I whistled for Rex then checked another box off the house agreement checklist I kept on the fridge. "I'm going to burn the sage again, a whole truckload this time."

As the familiar sound of dog claws along the hardwood sounded, I felt another presence, and I remembered we had a guest. I felt guilty for yelling at my ex in front of her. But then, it wasn't the first time my ex-husband and I had done that. In fact arguing in front of company and almost demanding they take sides was pretty much our MO back in the day.

"I'm sorry to intrude," the timid voice said, making me instantly feel sorry for her.

"Allow me to introduce our guest," Jackson said. A woman appeared with dark bobbed hair, full eyebrows, and a cute button nose. She was dressed in a sleek navy blue skirt and a polkadot sleeveless shirt. She was absolutely stunning.

"Carly, this is Gloria Elenore Thomas, our newest client," he said.

The girl smiled softly at me, hands behind her back as she nervously hover-rocked back and forth. She couldn't have been older than 18, max.

I searched my brain for something appropriate to say. "Sorry about your accident," I managed. "I mean, if it was an accident."

She nodded. "It wasn't."

"Let's go into the dining room and you can tell me everything you remember."

I knew it wasn't going to matter much, as far as the story's accuracy went. Ghosts didn't always remember things correctly after they died. It was only when we joined forces during a channeling that we relived the memory, exactly as it happened at the time it happened, second by second.

I pulled open the top drawer of the credenza in the back of the dining room, grabbed my notebook and pencil, then sat down.

"I don't know where to begin," she said.

"Gloria wasn't a regular on Landover Lake," Jackson said. "She's from California."

"Los Angeles," she chimed in, looking up at the ceiling like she was trying to remember. "We always rented a house on the lake, every summer since I was six, for two weeks with my aunt's family. My mother and my aunt grew up in Wisconsin, so even though we all lived in California, we always went to the lake to vacation." She sat on the chair next to me, such a small spirit, one I suspected was pretty easily taken advantage of in her day.

She continued. "I looked forward to it every year, eating fresh-picked corn while we caught fireflies and fished. I have to say, we were much more successful at catching fireflies than fish."

I nodded along, not much to take notes on yet. "So, the night you passed away. You were renting on the lake? What happened?"

"My cousin Nettie is what happened. Annette, but everyone called her Nettie. We'd both just graduated. Most years we kept to ourselves, just our families on the lake. But that year, Nettie got it in her head she wanted a boyfriend. A summer fling, she'd said. And the boys on the lake were so cute I found myself wanting that too. The boys only liked Nettie, of course. She'd just dyed her hair, like Marilyn Monroe's."

I wrote Nettie's name into my notebook along with a short description.

Gloria squinted her eyes up. "Honestly, I don't remember too much from the night itself. We went to the sock hop at the dance hall. Nettie found a boy and ditched me like always. I'd just turned 18 and this was my first country club dance. But I didn't really know anyone, so I was happy when the party broke up early. I wanted to go home."

"So the party ended early, huh?" I asked, scribbling as I talked. "Why?"

She looked at the ceiling. "Somebody spiked the punch and some kids were getting out of control, I think. I don't really remember. Nettie wasn't ready to go home, though. I do remember that. She convinced me to sneak on a boat with her. Man, it was the largest, most luxurious boat I'd ever been on, with a downstairs and everything. We thought the people on the boat would be cranked to have us along for their after-party. But I only remember their faces when they found us. They went ape, and not in a good way. I woke up in the water with Nettie."

"You're sure you didn't fall overboard?"

"Oh no. I don't remember how we got in the water, but it wasn't a fall. And when we were there, treading water, another boat showed up and yelled to us over a megaphone or something. I tried to wave my arms to get their attention, but when I looked up, the boat was coming right for us..."

I wrote as fast as I could at this point. These girls hadn't been partiers who met with an unfortunate accident. Something else had gone on entirely, and I was going to figure it out.

"So, will you help me?" she asked. Her voice seemed weaker now, her body almost completely transparent.

"Absolutely," I said. "Tomorrow morning, I'm going to find out everything I can about this so-called accident. We'll start gathering evidence, schedule a channeling of that night as soon as you're up for it. And if there's anyone left from that boat still alive today, they're going to wish they were dead. Mark my words."

I was feeling especially confident for someone who had no idea where she was going with this.

Gloria vanished, and I continued writing out our schedule and my plan to help her.

Jackson hovered by my side, reading over my shoulder in that annoying way he always did, even when we were married. "That's a lot of channeling you've got planned. Are you sure you're up for that?"

"Of course," I said in my most confident voice.

I knew he was concerned about the effects the channelings were starting to have on me. Truth was, I was concerned too. But I was also starting to feel drawn to them. I needed those channelings, and the ill effects that went with them. Possible hallucinations. White specks impeding my vision. Dizziness. The whole thing was like an intoxicating package that needed me to unwrap it, again and again.

I pulled the shoe box off the bookshelf in the living room and sat down at the coffee table. It was where I kept all the research I'd done on the crows and the history of Gate House. All the articles from 1954 about skull-crushing birds with thick yellowed beaks. And my notes. If anyone told me anything about Gate House, shapeshifters, curses, the Dead Forest, or birds, I put it in there, along with the things I remembered from every channeling and seance. I didn't have much so far.

There seemed to be a curse, all right, and I felt like I was supposed to end it somehow. But that was about as much as I knew, except for the fact I looked exactly like the woman who put the curse on the house in the first place. No idea why, but a coincidence didn't really seem possible.

My mother wouldn't tell me anything about my biological parents or my adoption, except to say the lawyer in the case resembled the lawyer I had now, a man who didn't seem to age, and kind of looked like he'd just stepped off the field of a Civil War reenactment.

Every week I'd think of some other thing to research, some other key word that might unlock the mystery behind this curse and my life, so I'd head optimistically over to the library.

But Parker's grandmother Mildred had been right. There wasn't nearly enough coverage in Potter Grove about the things that mattered, the supernatural things that terrorized this town. And might be back.

But with Gloria's help, I was about to do my own firsthand research and see things for myself in real time.

THANK you for checking out Behind the Boater's Cover-Up, available now on Amazon.

MORE BOOKS

BY ETTA FAIRE

Must Love Murder: A Sketchy Matchmaker Mystery, book one

P.S. I Poisoned You: A Sketchy Matchmaker Mystery, book two

Rockin' Around the Killing Spree: A Sketchy Matchmaker Mystery, book three

Over My Dead Husband's Body: A Ghosts of Landover Mystery, book one

After the Suffragette's Suicide: A Ghosts of Landover Mystery, book two

Behind the Boater's Cover-Up: A Ghosts of Landover Mystery, book three

Under the Cheater's Table: A Ghosts of Landover Mystery, book four

Made in the USA
Coppell, TX
31 December 2019

13932951R00114